A Sinful Gift

Emma Castle

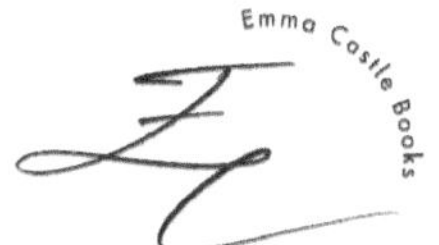

For everyone who's ever dreamed of being taken by that jerk you didn't want to admit you liked...and being shared with his best friend.

A Note from Emma Castle

Hello!

I'm so glad you here, truly. Thank you for choosing to read *A Sinful Gift*. This is a novella and yes, that means it is short, but I hope you'll enjoy the naughty ride it takes you on!

Sometimes when I'm writing deeply emotional, hard to write about topics, or torturing my beloved characters, I like to take a brief break and just do something sexy and fun. That's what this novella turned out to be, a lovely break from the intensity of other projects. It's meant to be enjoyed over a lunch break, or right before bed, or any other time you just need need a minute to escape somewhere fun with two yummy book boyfriends.

As always, I'm glad and honored you've taken a chance on my story and I hope you like it!

With love,

Emma Castle

Chapter One

Tonight, Hazel Callahan was a goddess of war, and she deserved to celebrate her victory.

Hazel grinned as she slipped onto a stool at her favorite little bar in Manhattan, the Golden Lair. It was one of those dark speakeasy clubs that required a new password each week to get in. Sexy, sleek, modern designs with a dash of glitzy 1920s art deco made it the perfect place to celebrate her big win. She had done the unthinkable. She'd beaten her longtime legal nemesis in an epic contract negotiation.

Blake London—her gorgeous, rich, and so impossibly arrogant opposing counsel—had been forced to concede to her client's requirements on a real estate contract. The negotiations had been intense over the last two months. Blake's scorching blue eyes had practically burned a hole into the table when he'd realized she'd outmaneuvered him and he finally had to tell his clients to accept her company's terms. Watching her old law school nemesis tell his clients his legal advice was for them to acquiesce to her demands made the last two months worth it.

"What can I get you?" the young woman tending the bar asked as she reached the corner where Hazel had tucked herself in. Hazel liked sitting where she could watch everyone in the bar come and go. People-watching was one of her favorite pastimes, and this bar always had the most fascinating people in it.

"A chocolate martini?" Hazel rarely splurged on cocktails, but tonight was a hell of a good night to indulge.

"Sure thing, hon." The bartender turned away to prepare her drink, and Hazel closed her eyes, replaying every glorious detail of taking the wind out of Blake London's sails.

He was a partner in one of the other biggest law firms in Manhattan, and he often ended up across the table from Hazel, usually in business negotiations. Neither of them was in court that often. As corporate attorneys, they both focused more on business deals rather than lawsuits. He might be a partner at one of the toughest law firms in Manhattan now, but their shared history had begun in law school at Pepperdine. They'd fought tooth and nail against each other for the top position in their class every year for three years. Back then, they'd come out pretty evenly, but each of her victories was a point he'd had to acknowledge. Even though they were six years out of law school, their academic rivalry was stronger than ever when they faced each other across a negotiation table.

"Thought I'd find you here," a smooth, dark voice said, interrupting her daydreaming.

Hazel's eyes flew open, and she turned to find none other than Blake himself sliding onto a stool beside her.

"What are you doing here, London?"

His sensual lips kicked up into an arrogant grin that made every woman, even her, feel torn between wanting to slap him or kiss him.

"You didn't think I'd let you off that easy tonight, Counselor," he teased, his voice holding a hint of mischief underlaid with the primal darkness that always gave her delicious shivers.

He was dangerous. *Too dangerous.* She knew that intimately, because she'd made the mistake of surrendering to him one night in their first year of law school. He had fucked her hard and dirty, pistoning into her with a raw strength that had left her thighs shaking. She might have survived that, but then he'd grinned at her, the same way he was doing now, and praised her as his good girl, and she'd been flooded with so much pleasure she was sure she'd never stop coming. Sex like that was too overwhelming. She was a woman with her own mind and her own life, and she wasn't about to let a man like Blake London own her body and soul through mind-blowing sex.

"Fuck off. I won this round," she reminded him, and before he could reply, the bartender brought her chocolate martini.

"What about you, handsome?" The bartender gazed at Blake with stars in her eyes. Hazel couldn't blame her. The man was the walking definition of sex and sin. A girl could climax if she stared too long at his chiseled features and those electric-blue eyes. She wanted to fist her hands in his rich, chocolate-dark hair, which always seemed to be styled to look slightly windblown, as if he spent the afternoons on a yacht in the south of France. It was unfair how attractive a man could look with so little effort.

"Scotch on the rocks. Glenlivet," he specified. He turned his focus back on Hazel as if the bartender never existed. She gave him credit for that.

"You won, Callahan," he conceded as he removed his dark-blue suit coat and slung it over the empty stool on his other side. His white dress shirt probably cost four times more than the burgundy knit dress she wore that she'd bought at a Black Friday sale. Damn, he looked good. The shirt was just snug enough to cling to his lean but powerfully muscled body. He wasn't a hulk, but the man was cut and strong enough to lift her up like she weighed nothing. She remembered that all too well —how easily he'd lifted her up and pinned her against the door of his apartment.

"And you lost." She sipped her martini and licked her lips at the delicious flavors in the alcohol. It was like drinking dessert.

"I lost to *you*," Blake murmured softly.

His gaze landed on her face, but she refused to look at him. It was dangerous to make eye contact with a man who had the power to eye-fuck a woman in the best way. But it was also his words. The way he'd said, *I lost to you* . . . as if he would only ever concede victory to *her*, and somehow that made the rush of pleasure all the more heady.

"I don't really care what turns you on, London," she replied coolly.

"Don't you?" He leaned in, pinning her further against the wall she sat by. It shouldn't have turned her on to get cornered like that, but it did. "You did care once, Callahan. And God, you were so fucking perfect that night. All that red hair spilling around your shoulders while you sucked me off on your knees. Then when I bent you over my desk . . . Babe, that was the hardest I've ever fucked a woman in my life, and you took it like such a good girl."

Oh God . . . Hazel clamped her thighs together as a cramping pain of pure, harsh lust twisted in her lower belly, forming a knot. The man knew just what to say to remind her how wanting him actually hurt.

"I haven't thought about that night in six years," she lied.

Those lips she dreamed about far too often flirted with a smile as he watched her.

"*Liar.*" He whispered the word as if it turned him on even more that she was attempting and *failing* to deny the electric charge that existed between them. Their gazes locked, and she knew she couldn't hide her reaction to the memory of that night they'd shared and how often she'd touched herself at night and cried out his name.

His blue eyes sharpened, brightened, as he seemed to read some hint of surrender in her expression. "Come home with me tonight."

"No," she replied, fighting to ignore the pounding of her heart against her ribs. Even though her body screamed, *Yes, God, yes!* She somehow found the strength to say, "Go home, London."

He leaned in to say something more, but a sudden hulking presence behind them had Blake halting.

"Is this guy bothering you, sweetheart?" a deep, gravelly voice asked.

Both she and Blake turned to look at the absolute mountain of a man standing behind them. He was fair-haired, with a faint tan and stunning brown eyes that were currently fixed in a stone-cold glare at London.

"He . . . Um . . ." Hazel couldn't think past how hot the stranger was. She never imagined she'd ever meet a man who could give Blake a run for his money in the looks department. But this man . . . He had that all-American, classic boy-next-door look, but he was built like a tank. Her gaze dropped instantly to his hips, which were narrow.

She gave herself a mental shake to try to free herself of the sudden image of a man this size between her thighs, pounding her into oblivion. Hazel took a drink and licked the chocolate off her lips. It had to be the martini. Chocolate always made her think about sex.

Her self-appointed rescuer wore dark blue jeans, work boots, and a black-and-blue flannel shirt. He looked like a sexy lumberjack come to life. There was a boyish charm to him, even though his hard and chiseled features were intensely masculine. She didn't see men like this in the Golden Lair that often . . . maybe not ever. Most men who came to this bar were like Blake, wearing expensive suits, reeking of high-dollar cologne. This man stood close enough that she could breathe in his scent. No cologne, just a clean, masculine scent with a hint of soap that smelled like pine.

"Tell him I'm not bothering you, Callahan," Blake ordered, his tone quiet but hard.

The mountain man's gaze cut to Hazel, searching her eyes. "I don't mind throwing trash out. You give the word and he's gone, sweetheart." The way he said *sweetheart* wasn't patronizing like it would be from most men who didn't know her. No, when he said it, it felt like a true endearment, as though he was the sort of man who saw every woman in his life as sweet, and the word came from a place of affection.

Damn . . .

Blake, never the type to back down from a fight, pushed off his stool and stood toe to toe with the other man. They were of a similar height. An electric charge shot between them, a violent aura of two males in their prime ready to kill over a female. Until that moment, Hazel never thought she would like the idea of anyone fighting over her, but something about these two men sent a flood of wet heat between her thighs, forcing her to squeeze her legs together and self-consciously tug at the hem of her dress.

"Ma'am?" The man's gravelly voice raked deliciously over her skin, and her nipples pebbled at the sound.

"Um . . ." Why was she having trouble speaking? She was a lawyer; speaking was her job. But damned if she wasn't tongue-tied by this entire situation.

"Callahan," Blake warned, and she recognized that voice. It held a warning.

The last time he'd used that voice, he'd had her bottom in the air, spanking it hard enough it brought tears to her eyes and made her beg for more, more of him, more of all the dark, sinful pleasures only he seemed to know how to awaken in her.

"I think the lady's hesitation means you need to take a walk." The man jerked his head toward the front door of the club.

Blake stared at him for a long moment, and Hazel held her breath. Blake had every right to be confident. He was a fighter, a man who could hold his own in a fistfight just as easily as he did in boardrooms and courtrooms. But wisely, he chose not to fight her rescuer tonight.

"Fine." Blake's hard stare softened as he looked at Hazel. "As promised this afternoon, you will have my client's signed contract in your inbox tomorrow morning." He was once more focused on business, and Hazel breathed a sigh of relief when he put on his coat. He threw back the rest of his whiskey in a hard gulp, set the glass down, and without a glance at the mountain man, left the bar.

"Asshole," the flannel-wearing man said as he took a seat a few stools away from Hazel and ordered an old-fashioned from the bartender.

"Thanks for the rescue," Hazel murmured to him.

"No problem. Some men need to learn that no means no, and when a woman wants to drink alone at a bar, that's her business and not an invitation."

Hazel chuckled. "You sound like a Boy Scout."

The man flashed her a boyish grin that hit her behind the knees. "Eagle Scout, ma'am." He gave her the three-fingered Boy Scout salute. A blush worked its way up her neck to her face, and she nearly asked him about all the different knots he could tie around a girl. But she stopped herself just in time. Damn, this martini was working some black magic in her.

The man left her alone to enjoy her drink. The silence was pleasant. Sometimes a man expected to get something from a woman for saving her from a bad situation. But this guy didn't. He was a perfect gentleman.

By the time she finished her drink, she was feeling a

bit lightheaded. It was entirely her fault for ordering a cocktail without any dinner. She used her phone to call a cab and then stood, wavering a little on her feet.

"You okay, sweetheart?" The man caught her elbow as she clutched the bar with her other arm to steady herself. She wasn't drunk, but she was definitely buzzed.

"Yeah. I don't drink that often, and I really should have had something to eat before ordering that martini."

"You should wait here and sober up," he advised. "I can have the bartender get you a bottle of water."

"No, it's okay. I called a cab." She bit her lip, staring at the front door. What were the chances that Blake might be waiting out front to talk to her again? Probably minimal, but she didn't want to risk it.

"Would you mind walking me to my car? The cab should be here in a couple of minutes to pick me up." She retrieved her phone and texted the driver to meet her at the rear entrance of the bar instead of out front.

"You want to go out the back?" The man's blond hair fell into his eyes as he studied the exit door skeptically.

"Yes. I told my cabdriver to meet me there. You don't mind walking with me, do you?"

"Not at all," he agreed, and stood. She collected her clutch purse and paid her tab. Then she let the man escort her to the back door.

The alley out back was dark and a little chilly, but Hazel breathed a sigh of relief when she saw a waiting car a few yards away. When they reached the vehicle, she turned to thank the man, but she gasped as he pulled her into the dark shadow of the building.

"I—" She started to speak and lifted one hand to push against his chest to force him to step back a little. But he didn't budge.

She had no chance to react as the man suddenly captured her wrist with one large hand. He twisted something soft and silky around it and then tied it to her other wrist. Fucking Boy Scout—he'd tied some fancy knot she couldn't pull free from!

"Hey, what are you—" Before she could scream, he pressed a wadded cloth into her mouth, gagging her. She struggled, but the martini was still making her head a bit dizzy. The terror was slow to come, but once it began to build, her heart thrashed against her ribs.

The man opened the car door with ease, scooped her up, and deposited her in the back seat. She tried to wriggle toward the door, but he shut it, preventing her escape. When he got into the front seat, he hit the door-lock button.

This wasn't the cab she'd hired. It was *his* car. He was kidnapping her. All of these realizations built inside her as she tried to free her hands, and failing at that, she tugged uselessly at the car door handle.

With the martini still making her woozy, she made a muffled sound of protest against the gag.

"Easy, sweetheart," he murmured.

She let out another cry for help.

"I promise, no one's going to hurt you," the mountain man said. "I'm taking you to an old friend. You're the perfect gift for him."

Chapter Two

"*You're the perfect gift for him.*"

The man's words echoed in Hazel's mind as she stared bleakly out the car window. How had this happened to her? She'd been such a fool. She wished she had gone home with Blake. At least then she would be safe. Blake was a sexy asshole, but he would never hurt her.

She wasn't sure how long they were in the car, but after they left Manhattan, she dozed off in the back seat, thanks to the martini. She was still a little groggy when she came awake to find herself in the mountain man's arms again. He held her gently cradled against his chest as he strode up the steps to a beautiful mansion. The earthy scent that clung to him smelled like fresh-cut timber. Beneath all of that there was a softer, more male scent that belonged solely to him, and Hazel felt intensely and intimately aware of him as that aroma filled her head. His palms were calloused, and his fingers felt firm as he cradled her legs and her upper back, but not rough enough to bruise.

She made a soft sound against the gag, but he ignored her. The front door opened as they approached, and an older man in a black suit stared solemnly at them.

"Good evening, Mr. Wilde," the man at the door said.

Mr. Wilde. Hazel looked up at the face of the man who carried her. Wilde. The name suited him. He seemed like some ancient wood god who had stepped out of a thousand-year-old forest and now walked among mortals for the first time.

When her captor noticed her staring up at him, he shot her a boyish grin before he addressed the man at the door.

"Evening, Chalmers. I have a gift for him, if he's home."

"I believe the master will enjoy her. Please come with me." Chalmers offered Wilde an amused smile as he carried her down the hall to a pair of large oak doors.

What she glimpsed, briefly, of the house made her think that it might be one of those old oil baron mansions she'd toured on the Gold Coast of Long Island. Yet the furnishings were sleek, modern. Everything had an understated elegance that spoke of money without being flashy. Whoever lived here had nothing to prove to anyone and seemed to just enjoy beauty. There were works of art on the walls, high vaulted ceilings, brilliantly lit chandeliers, and some rooms they passed had color schemes that seemed to come out of an interior designer's fairy tale.

"The library, eh? He must be in a mood," Wilde mused.

"Yes, he is. But I believe your gift will cheer him up." The servant chuckled, as if all of this was entirely normal. Then he left them alone and walked back down the hall.

Hazel's heart pounded wildly as the mountain man carried her into a vast library that had rows of shelves containing hundreds of books. At the far end of the room, a trio of wingback chairs faced the fireplace. A fire was lit, and it cracked and popped in an otherwise silent room that felt charged with a strange and exciting sort of energy. Hazel glimpsed a man's hand resting on the arm of one of the chairs.

The master . . . It had to be. She noticed his sleeve had been rolled up, exposing a swath of tan skin. The muscles of his forearm moved as he swirled a glass of amber-colored liquor. Something about the intimacy of the scene sent her blood pounding through her veins. She couldn't ignore the instinctive feminine desire that seeing a muscular male arm created in her.

"I have a present for you, old friend." Wilde's deep voice broke the silence.

Hazel lifted her head up to stare at him and made a soft whimpering sound, trying to plead with him.

"Hush, sweetheart, you'll like him. I know it," Wilde murmured to her.

She lowered her brows and tried to growl at him through the gag. This only made the bastard smile, as if he thought the sound was adorable.

The chair creaked and a man stood, silhouetted by the fire behind him as he downed the last of his drink and set the glass on a table. From his shape, Hazel could tell he was tall and well built. She wondered if his face was as beautiful as his silhouette hinted his body was. She *shouldn't* care, she should be screaming and fighting, but something in her, something dark and delicious, was stirring like a covetous dragon rolling on its bed of gold.

"Mason." The man spoke in a rich voice, and Hazel guessed that must be Wilde's first name. But that bit of knowledge was quickly overshadowed by the realization that this man, this *master's* voice was . . . familiar.

"I saw how much you wanted her tonight, and it's been a while since you've had a pet," Mason replied in his slightly gravelly voice.

"How you spoil me, old friend." The silhouetted man stepped forward, and Hazel gasped against her gag as his face was suddenly illuminated by the light of a nearby lamp.

It was Blake. The kidnapper had brought her to Blake. She was torn between fury and relief, briefly followed by confusion. The two men had appeared to be strangers at the bar and had nearly come to blows over her. Yet now they were old friends?

"Hello, Hazel," Blake said as he approached her. Mason set her down on her feet but kept his hands firmly on her shoulders, holding her in place. She glared at Blake as he reached out with his fingers to gently pry the gag from her mouth.

"London, you ass!"

"Hush," Blake commanded gently. "You're in no danger, Hazel. You *know* me."

"This *jerk* kidnapped me!" She rammed her elbow

hard into Mason's stomach, and to her immense satisfaction, he grunted.

"Mason is an old childhood friend. You'll have to forgive him his rough ways. He sees something he knows I want, and he acquires it for me. He's thoughtful that way."

She snorted. "Well, the joke's over. I want to leave now," Hazel stated.

Blake and Mason shared a silent, intense look, and she wondered if they had the ability to read each other's minds.

"No, Hazel. I think you'll be staying for a while," Blake finally said. "Watching you win this afternoon, touching you at the lounge tonight . . . I realized that one night in law school of fucking you to within an inch of your life wasn't enough. I want to hear you screaming my name while you're coming around my cock." He smiled, and her mouth went dry at his words.

"Actually, let me amend that, Counselor." He brushed her hair back from her face and cupped the back of her neck, his fingers fisting in her hair. "I don't want it—I need it. And I think you do too."

His words, so possessively spoken, should have terrified her, but this was Blake. She did actually know him, that rich, arrogant bad boy she'd fallen for in law school. He was a heartbreaker, irresistible, *perfect*. There wasn't a sane woman alive who wouldn't go mad to have him, and that included her.

"One week. One week during which I will make you come harder than you've ever come before," Blake murmured as he moved his hand to cup her chin. "Belong to me for seven nights and let me convince you that you want to stay forever." He paused, his electric eyes sending sparks through her body. "And then, after . . . If you want to leave, I'll let you go."

No, she thought. This was how it started. If she let him have even one night, let alone seven, she might fall over that last precipice into the abyss that was loving this man—and she'd lose herself forever.

Blake brushed his thumb over her bottom lip, his blue eyes hot with white fire while he stared at her mouth as if it would save his soul.

"What do you have to lose?" Blake asked her.

My heart, she thought. That was why she'd run from him in the first place.

"Be my good girl again, Hazel. Your bed's been cold too long and so has mine. You deserve to have a man fucking you in the way you need, the way you deserve, don't you, baby?"

He had known what she needed that night. He had dominated her, pleasured her until she'd screamed so much her throat turned raw. He'd taken away all her worries and her fears, shown her how beautiful and desirable she was and that she was wonderful for trusting him and submitting to him. The power to say yes or no had always been hers, and they both knew it.

He watched her face, his eyes holding hers as he seemed to hear her inner thoughts, but he said nothing. He waited patiently like he had all the time in the world.

She stared at his mouth, knowing how exquisite his lips would feel on her flesh, and trailed her gaze down to his slightly open dress shirt. His tie was missing, and a hint of dark chest hair showed on his skin. She glanced down at her hands, seeing the fabric around her wrists and realizing it was a necktie. It was not one he had worn today, but it was one she recognized as his.

"Did you plan this?" she asked, lifting her bound hands to show him the tie around her wrists. Somehow Mason had it with him tonight to use when he'd kidnapped her from the bar. Surely they hadn't orchestrated this whole thing together?

Blake gently captured her wrists, studying the necktie she showed him.

"I didn't plan this, no, but Mason visits my house often. Did you steal this?" he asked the other man.

Mason laughed, and faint lines crinkled at the

corners of his eyes, making Hazel realize he must smile and laugh often. "I did."

"You did well," Blake said. "You know, Hazel, Mason and I were supposed to meet for drinks tonight, even though I knew it was your night to drink there. But then he defended you, and I left with my tail firmly between my legs, which quite ruined my night. I was afraid you might go home with him rather than me."

Now Mason was the one who chuckled. "I wanted her to be a surprise for you."

Hazel stared at Mason, then at Blake, feeling like a kitten caught between two large wolves.

"You weren't really going to fight?" She was oddly relieved. As much as she'd been initially aroused by the idea, now she didn't want to see them fight over her, even though she was still pissed as hell that Mason had just grabbed her from the bar like some creepy stalker.

"Never. We are as close as brothers," Mason said.

"Great," Hazel muttered. She tried to pull free of the gentle but firm weight of Mason's hands still on her shoulders.

"Hazel." Blake murmured her name in a way that reminded her of midnight whispers and silk sheets sliding against skin. "What's it to be? One week with me?" he asked.

"I've got work . . ." She tried to think of any excuse.

"Mason will retrieve your laptop and any work files you need, but I want you here. So I can have access to you whenever I want. But I know for a fact you were going to take a week off soon, for vacation. I'm sure if you called your paralegal tomorrow, she could handle things until you got back."

She arched a brow. He was right. She had been planning to fly to some hot island and lie on a beach beneath palm trees. "What about me and what *I* want?"

His lips kicked up in that grin that had captured her heart in law school.

"You'll have access to me too. Anytime you want me, *I'm yours, Hazel.*"

I'm yours. Such simple words, yet they made her dizzy like she'd drunk champagne too quickly. One of the smartest, sexiest lawyers in New York City, who could have anyone he wanted . . . had just said he'd be hers. *Oh God . . .*

"I . . ." She was tongue-tied, but as always Blake seemed to know just what to do to win her over. That was what made him so dangerous.

He moved closer, pressing her back against Mason, trapping her between the two of them so she had no escape as he fisted a hand in her hair at the base of her neck. Then he kissed her. *Hard.* It was a delicious, overwhelming assault on her senses as she tasted scotch and sin on his lips. It only added to the burning intensity of the moment.

His tongue plunged between her lips and decadently flicked against hers, mimicking the thrusting of lovemaking. His fingers tightened slightly in her hair, creating a whisper of pain that she liked, and it made her whimper against his mouth. He kissed her even more ruthlessly now, seeming determined to erase any resistance she might have left to him. She was all too aware of his hardness and the mirrored hardness of Mason behind her. She couldn't escape, but did she even want to?

When he finally let her breathe, she panted softly, her lips feeling bruised from his kisses.

"Give yourself to me," he commanded in a rough whisper. "You know I'll take care of my good girl, won't I?" She saw his control was fraying. God, she loved knowing she could make him lose control like that.

"Y—yes," she replied.

His lips curved and he cupped her cheek in one palm. "Good girl. There's just one more thing . . ."

"What?"

"Mason and I share *everything.*"

She blinked, dazed as she tried to process what he'd said. "Share? Share what?"

"*You.* For the next week, you're not just mine. You're

his too. Now show Mason what a good girl you are for him." He turned her toward Mason, and she stared up at the chiseled hardness of the blond-haired giant. Mason's expression was one of raw hunger, the kind that promised a violent rush of pleasure if she gave herself over to it . . . to him. He would fuck her hard, would make her see stars, and oh God, she needed that more than anything in that moment.

His calloused fingers gently captured her chin and tilted her face up as he lowered his head. For such a fierce man, his kiss began softly, almost sweetly, yet there was an underlying carnality to it that made her shiver deliciously. As if emboldened by her response, he parted her lips with his tongue and kissed her, slowly, seductively, with a surprising sensuality that she did not expect from a man like this.

She moaned, unable to resist reacting to him as desire throbbed between her thighs. Blake's hand slid around her waist, holding her tight against him from behind as he whispered in her ear.

"Just imagine taking the both of us, being surrounded by us, *filled* by us. How would you like that?" He flicked his tongue into the shell of her ear, and she felt his hardness press against her lower back. "We would leave no part of you untouched and unloved. You would be worshipped like the goddess you are and claimed as our prize."

She wouldn't like it. She would *love* it. But she would probably die from an overload of pleasure.

She whimpered as Blake cupped her breasts, kneading them gently and lightly pinching her nipples.

"I want you out of this fucking dress," he growled, and the primal anger in his voice at her clothing daring to come between her body and his made her tremble with excitement. She'd always liked it when he got a little rough in his eagerness.

"Strip her," Mason urged him. "I need to see this little beauty bared to me." Then Mason was kissing her again, that soft mouth of his now hard and hungry on hers.

Blake's hands tore at the zipper on the back of her dress as he yanked it down and tugged it free of her body. She wore only a lacy pale-pink bra with matching panties beneath the dress. Whenever she faced off against Blake in a business deal, she liked to secretly wear her sexiest lingerie. It felt like her secret superpower, because the way he looked at her made her certain he knew exactly what she wore beneath her elegant suits and dresses. And the feral gleam in the polished lawyer's eyes made her wet.

"You always know how to bring out the caveman in

me," Blake whispered harshly against her skin before he bit into the soft flesh at the crook of her neck.

His hands roved over her belly, her hips, and back up to her breasts, first cupping them and then pinching her nipples lightly through the thin lace.

Mason's mouth still moved over hers, trapping her focus on him as he gripped her shoulders with those large warm hands. The coarse fabric of Mason's jeans rubbed against her bare thighs, and he nudged her legs apart so that she was forced to ride his leg, rubbing her clit through her panties against his hard quads.

Blake's expensive suit felt soft as silk against her skin along her back. He continued to flick his tongue against her ear and nibble at her neck, as though he wanted to leave a mark. When Mason ran his fingers through her hair and tugged gently on the strands in tandem with Blake lightly pinching her nipples, it was too much.

She wasn't ready for Blake's sensual assault, not with Mason's mouth so hungrily ravishing hers. She came suddenly, hard, like a grenade detonating with no warning.

"Shit, she just came from a damn kiss," Mason growled against her lips. His hands cupped her face and he stared into her eyes, absorbing her expression as pleasure rolled through her body. She stared back at him, utterly enraptured by the cinnamon fire of Mason's brown eyes.

"She's always been so responsive. It's why she's such a good girl for me, and now she'll be a good girl for you too." Blake's exploring fingers stroked along the tops of her breasts, flirting with the lines of the lace cups of her bra. Her nipples turned into even harder diamond points. She desperately wanted a mouth sucking on them, but she was still shaking from the surprise orgasm and her speech was limited as she slowly descended from her height of pleasure.

"I think our pet needs to be in bed," Blake said, seeming to notice her legs trembling even though she was partially braced against one of Mason's thighs.

Our pet. The way he said that, the way he was happy to share her with Mason, was the most erotic thing she'd ever heard in her life. She'd always had fantasies about being shared between two men.

"Take her up to my bedroom," Blake told Mason. "I'll grab her clothes."

Mason scooped her up in his arms as though she weighed nothing at all. She wasn't tiny, but she could get used to being carried around like this. She curled her arms around Mason's neck and felt his muscles harden beneath her fingertips. He walked out of the library and down the hall to a bedroom at the back of the large mansion.

A massive four-poster king-size bed stood against one wall. It had crisp white sheets and dark-green accent pillows. String lights twined around the posts and trailed in lines down the back of the massive carved mahogany headboard. There was a hint of romanticism in the setup that made her feel oddly comforted and excited at the same time. She hadn't expected Blake to have a bedroom like this. Pale-green vines had been painted on the cream-colored walls, making the room feel a little bit like a garden, yet it was completely masculine.

Mason set her down on the bed and turned to Blake as he joined them. He had retrieved her dress from the floor, along with her clutch purse, which Mason had carried in from the car when they'd first arrived. He set them both on top of the dresser, next to a black-and-silver box, open to reveal a row of expensive wristwatches. When he turned to face her, he absently twisted the signet ring on his left pinkie finger, which caught her attention.

The night he had taken her to bed in law school, that signet ring had left imprints all over her hips from where he'd gripped her hard while railing her from behind. She had loved every faint mark from that ring, because they had been marks of his possession. She closed her thighs, aware of how dripping wet she was as the two men stood side by side facing her.

"How the hell did you ever let her go?" Mason asked Blake.

Blake nodded, his gaze burning into hers. "Yes, the one that got away. I didn't know she'd run, or I would have tied her to my bed and seduced her into staying with me forever."

"Well she's not going anywhere now." Mason flashed that boyish grin and reached for the buttons of his flannel shirt. "You're ours now, sweetheart. Blake may have let you go, but *I* won't. Once you've had me inside you, you'll never want to leave."

If any other man besides one of the two in this room had said that, she would have laughed at their egos, but she believed Mason. She'd only had a taste of him so far, but that single, explosive taste told her that he would own her just as Blake had. She scooted back a little on the massive bed, suddenly very aware of how nearly naked she was in front of two men intent on fucking the life out of her. She shivered as she watched them share a knowing glance that charged the room with even more awareness of what was to happen between the three of them. Her skin flushed and she swallowed hard, noticing the bulge in Mason's jeans.

He was big, like Blake. *Oh God* . . . Could she even take them both?

She should run, get the hell out of there before she lost herself to these two men, but as she watched Blake unbutton his dress shirt while Mason peeled his flannel shirt off his darkly bronzed skin, she knew what her fate would be. No more running. If she had a week with them, she wanted to make every minute count. She wouldn't think about what would happen when their seven days were over. There was only this . . . only pleasure.

Chapter Three

Blake's heart beat hard as he stared down at the most beautiful woman he'd ever had the pleasure of taking to his bed. She had run from him, but he wasn't going to let her get away again. Not when the chemistry between them was hot enough to set them both on fire. The only thing that made this more electric to his senses was the hunger in his best friend's eyes. Blake never shared anything that belonged to him . . . except with Mason. They hadn't lied to Hazel: they were as close as brothers after all they'd been through over the years. It was hard to explain, but while he had no physical attraction to Mason, he enjoyed seeing his friend experience pleasure, *especially* with Hazel. It felt right, the three of them together like this. And now his friend would taste the sweetness of

Hazel Callahan and it would change Mason forever, just as it had changed Blake.

"Kiss her," Blake said.

Mason's lips kicked into a grin. "Gladly."

He walked around to the other side of the bed and came up behind her, naked except for his jeans. Blake licked his lips as Hazel tilted her head to look at Mason over her shoulder, hunger in her eyes. If he hadn't been watching so closely, he would have missed the flush of her skin that proved to him that she liked the way Mason stalked toward the bed and that she was into this predator-and-prey play. His feisty little Hazel was a spitfire when they faced off professionally, but in the bedroom? She was a kitten—sweet, fuckable, and adorable when she was hunted like this and caught. Then she became a firecracker that any man would die to hold on to, even if she burned him up.

While she was distracted by Mason stalking up to the bed, Blake gently grasped Hazel's ankles and pulled, sending her flying flat onto her back on the bed. She gasped, but before she could properly respond to Blake, Mason climbed onto the bed near her head and leaned over, kissing her upside down. A powerful shiver went through Blake's entire body as he heard Hazel groan. He saw Mason's tongue flick between her lips, and his hands captured her wrists and pinned them to the bed.

He and Mason had her between them now, utterly at their mercy, and they were going to enjoy every second of this.

Grinning, Blake hooked his fingers in the lace of her panties and dragged them off her body, baring her sweet sex to him. Then he knelt on the floor at the edge of the bed and pressed her thighs wide with his palms. He loved worshiping Hazel on his knees. It had been too long since he'd feasted on her. He took his time, pressing soft kisses into her inner thighs and the top of her mound before he flicked his tongue over her clit as it peeked out from its hood. She jerked at that little swish and swirl of his tongue, and she whimpered against Mason's mouth. Damn, there was nothing better than the sound of her muffled reactions while Mason kissed her.

Blake moved his mouth down to her slit. She was soaking wet, his good little girl. He dragged the flat of his tongue deep into her, lapping at her before sucking on her clit, and she writhed hard enough that he had to pin her knees flat on the bed to keep her open and still for his slow seduction. Between long, teasing licks, he lifted his head to watch Hazel and Mason kiss. She was completely surrendering to Mason's masterful attentions.

Blake had a wicked idea as her thighs trembled under his hands and he realized she was close to coming.

"Mason, give our girl something to suck on while she comes."

Mason gave one more sweet nuzzle against her lips before he pulled back to look down at her. "You want that, sweetheart? You want to suck me off while Blake tongues you?"

Her lovely hazel eyes were glazed with pleasure, and she nodded eagerly. Mason sat back on his heels on the bed and unfastened his jeans, letting his cock spring forth. He moved closer, cradling her head as she parted her lips and took him into her mouth.

"Fucking hell," Mason groaned at the first touch of her lips around the crown of his cock. When she took him deeper, his eyes rolled back in his head. Blake laughed softly, then slid two fingers into Hazel. She moaned around Mason's cock and tilted her hips, begging Blake to penetrate her deeper.

Mason lightly fisted a hand in her hair but didn't push her head toward him. He simply held on to her while she chose her own pace to torture him. Blake knew she was good at that, torturing a man with pleasure. Hell, *he* was tortured right now because he wanted to be inside her. But he had a rule with Hazel. His good girl always came first.

Mason threw his head back, the muscles in his neck straining as he fought off the need to come.

"Make her come, Blake," Mason demanded harshly. "I want her to scream around me."

Blake slid three fingers into her wetness and then curled his fingers to stroke the spot deep within that made her flinch and whimper. He continued thrusting and stroking, using his thumb from his other hand to rub circles over her clit.

"Come for us, baby," Blake breathed. "Let Mason feel you scream with pleasure."

She only made it two more strokes before she came. Her cry was muffled as she tried to take Mason deeper.

"Easy, sweetheart, I'm too big for that," he warned and pulled back, but Hazel tried to stop him by hooking her fingers in his jeans pocket and tugging him closer.

"I'm not gonna last," Mason warned Blake. "She's too fucking good at this."

"Take my spot." Blake nodded at where he stood between Hazel's parted thighs.

"You sure?" Mason moved away from Hazel, and she fell back onto the bed, gasping from her orgasm.

"Yeah, I am." Blake moved out of the way and crawled across the bed to lie beside Hazel. He cupped her face, turning her so she would meet his gaze.

"Mason's going to fuck you, baby, and I want to watch him do it."

A moment's uncertainty passed across Hazel's face.

"You don't want to—"

He understood what she feared, that he didn't want her enough to take her.

"Oh I do, baby. *I do.* But just like Mason gave you to me tonight as a gift, I want to give him *this* as a gift. I want to see him sink into you and feel your tight little body around him as he comes." Blake stroked his thumb over her bottom lip, and she licked his thumb, drawing it between her lips to suck on it. His cock strained against his pants, and he barely contained a moan. This woman knew his every weakness. He shot her a wolfish grin. "And then . . . it will be *my* turn."

Her eyes dilated with excitement, the hazel irises nearly swallowed by the black pupils. She wanted this, wanted him and Mason both. He could see it in her face as she glanced at Mason, now stroking her thighs with surprising gentleness.

"O—kay." She wriggled as Mason grasped his shaft and rubbed himself through her slick folds, coating his cock with her arousal.

"You ready for me, sweetheart?" Mason asked.

She nodded and fisted her hands in the bedding, bracing herself. Blake also nodded at Mason, and Mason slowly pushed into her body. Blake watched her take his friend's cock deep. She whimpered as Mason worked to fit into her.

"How long has it been for you, baby?" Blake stroked her cheek, concerned by her tightness.

"Two years," she confessed.

"Fuck," Mason groaned, and sank in another inch.

"Be careful with our girl, Mason," Blake cautioned, but he knew Mason would be. Mason withdrew a little, grasped Hazel's ass, and lifted her before thrusting in a little harder, sinking deeper until he was fully inside her.

"She feels like a fucking dream." Mason grunted as he withdrew and pumped in again. "Hazel, sweetheart, tell me I can go *harder . . . faster*," Mason groaned.

"Yes," she begged. "*Please . . .*"

* * *

Hazel didn't like to beg, but she needed Mason to go harder and faster. He lifted her legs up a little more and tightly curled strong hands around her thighs. A second later, he thrust into her so deeply, she saw stars. Once he began, he didn't let up, and she didn't want him to. He pounded into her, the smacking of their bodies heightening her excitement as the aftershocks of her previous climax began to intensify toward a new one. She rolled her head toward Blake, who still lay there on the bed beside her, his blue eyes fiery as he watched her face.

"Blake," she pleaded. "Please, I want . . ."

"Tell me what you want, baby," he encouraged as he stroked his thumb over her lips, tracing their shape.

"I want you to kiss me."

"How can I say no to such a good girl?" He leaned over her, his lips touching hers in a chaste kiss.

It wasn't enough. She wanted *more*. She reached up and dug her fingers into his wavy dark hair and flicked her tongue against the seam of his lips. He surrendered, parting his lips, and she deepened the kiss, giving them both what they needed.

Mason panted as he continued to ravish her, and she lost herself completely. There was nothing outside this room with these two men and the pleasure between them. She came so hard it felt like the entire earth broke apart beneath her. The walls she'd fought so hard to build around her heart began to fracture. She knew with a terrifying certainty that they would break through those walls soon.

Mason shouted with his own climax and drove so deeply she wasn't sure where she began and he ended. They were fused by passion, and the intensity of what they had just shared heightened everything. His release filled her, and she was dimly aware that they hadn't had the safe-sex talk. She was on birth control, but they still needed to talk about it.

Blake slowed his kiss and pulled away slightly. "I can feel you thinking, Hazel," he said. "What's the matter?"

"I . . . er . . . We didn't use a condom," she whispered, her gaze drifting to Mason's cock still buried in her as he stroked her knees tenderly.

"I'm clean. What about you, Mason?" Blake looked to his friend.

"The same. I got tested last week."

She breathed a sigh of relief. "Me too. And I have an IUD."

"So no condoms, then?" Blake asked her. "We'll use them if you want us to."

She shook her head. "No condoms, if we all agree."

"Agreed," Mason and Blake said in unison.

Blake leaned in and kissed her again. She felt Mason pull out of her, and a few moments later, a warm wet cloth was rubbed between her legs. She knew she would be a little sore tomorrow, but she didn't mind. Mason hadn't exactly been gentle, but she hadn't wanted him to be. She relaxed as Blake continued to kiss her, and then she felt herself slipping down that slope toward sleep.

Blake paused kissing her to chuckle gently.

"It takes just three orgasms to wear you out?" he teased. "No, baby, we have to work on your stamina."

She dug her nails lightly into his bare shoulder, but her reaction was softened by the yawn that she stifled.

"Poor kitten," Mason murmured. "She needs sleep."

"She does," Blake replied.

"But you didn't . . ." Hazel still felt oddly shy about sex with Blake even though he was breaking down her inhibitions.

"When I take you, I want you good and rested." Blake trailed the backs of his fingers over her cheek, and it only made her want sleep more because it felt so good.

"Hmmm . . ." She closed her eyes and sighed dreamily.

Damn Blake and his seductive ways.

"Why don't you put our girl to bed, Mason. I'm going to take a quick shower." Blake kissed her forehead and slid off the bed, leaving her and Mason alone.

She shyly closed her legs, which made Mason chuckle. He had buttoned up his jeans again, but he was still gloriously shirtless.

"I'll let you be shy tonight, sweetheart, but starting tomorrow, don't be. You're gorgeous and I don't want you to ever hide." He scooped her up in his arms, and she was gently set on her feet while he pulled back the covers of the bed for her. Then he opened one of the nightstand drawers and removed a soft, worn-looking T-shirt that said *Pepperdine* on it. She recognized it as one of Blake's old shirts from law school.

"Take off that bra and put this on," Mason said. "I'll go and get something for you to eat."

She removed her bra after he left and slipped the Pepperdine shirt over her head. The cotton was soft, and it came down to mid-thigh. She liked wearing Blake's shirt, but she liked it even more that it was also *her* school, not just Blake's.

Blake may have been a dominant lover in bed, but he never made her feel small. Feminine, yes. Delicate in the best way, hell yes. But he never diminished her or dimmed her shine, or belittled her accomplishments. That was what made him so dangerous. He was a forever kind of man, and she wasn't sure she was ready for that. Her work, like his, was demanding and challenging. But she liked it. Still, a secret part of her feared that giving in to him, being his, would make her soft. She wanted to spend all day in bed until she was passed out from life-changing orgasms. That didn't leave a lot of room for work, and she loved her work.

She snuggled in Blake's bed and listened to the shower sounds coming from the bathroom. If Blake knew anything about her, he knew when she needed a little space, like right now.

When Mason returned, he carried a tray of warm chocolate chip cookies, clearly fresh-baked, and a glass of cold milk.

"Milk and cookies? I'm not Santa Claus," she said, even though she immediately reached for the nearest cookie and the glass. She bit into the snack as Mason sat down beside her on the edge of the bed, watching her with an amused expression that left faint crinkles at the corners of his eyes. This was a man who smiled often.

"Oh my God, these are amazing." She could tell they were homemade.

"Among other things, I occasionally bake. The secret is extra vanilla and a pinch of brown sugar."

A man baking . . . It was strangely hot. Hazel swallowed a mouthful of the sinful cookie and then took a big gulp from her glass. It was whole milk, and it almost tasted like cream.

"You're going to fatten me up if I keep eating like this," she warned teasingly.

"You won't see me complaining," Mason said as he reached up and gently tucked a lock of hair behind her ear. Then he stood and leaned down, pressing a kiss to her lips. "Sleep well."

"You're leaving?" she asked. He was still a stranger to her, but she didn't want him to leave.

"I had your beautiful body tonight. That was my

treat. Blake's treat will be having you all to himself for the rest of the night. But don't get used to it. I plan to share a bed with you soon."

Soon . . . She was still staring at the doorway when Blake came out of the bathroom wrapped in nothing but a white towel that hung low on his hips. His dark hair was wet, and water droplets dewed on his skin. His lips twitched as he saw her holding half a cookie and staring at him.

"Ah, you've brought out Mason's domestic side, I see. He doesn't bake for just any woman."

"Who is he?" she asked as Blake walked over to his dresser and dropped the towel. His gloriously muscled ass was bare to her, and her mouth ran dry. She frantically took a big gulp of milk to wash the cookie down before she choked on it.

"Mason and I grew up together as boys. I was a rich kid, and he was from the trailer park. We had never really been friends before, but when some of the boys in sixth grade decided to beat me up, Mason fought those other three students off and saved me from what would have been a humiliating experience. After that we became inseparable. I helped him to find scholarships so he could get into Northwestern, and then when I went to Pepperdine, he moved to live near me. While you and I were in law school, he built up his own business, and he's done very well. I wasn't lying when I said we've become like brothers." Blake pulled on a pair of black pajama pants and faced her.

"What is his business?"

"Carpentry. He makes special pieces of furniture, even small boats. They sell for hundreds of thousands of dollars."

A carpenter. Well, that explained the work boots, jeans, and flannel.

"I thought he might be a lumberjack," she said.

Blake laughed. God, the sound made her belly quiver with excitement. He had the best laugh; it was so sexy and genuine, and she loved the way it rumbled from deep in his chest.

"Better not tell him that," Blake said. He turned off all the lights in the room save one, on the nightstand by her side of the bed. Then he slid in under the sheets beside her.

"Does he hate being called a lumberjack?" she asked as she ate another cookie. It would be a shame to waste them while they were still warm.

Blake leaned over her and stole a cookie from the plate. He chewed thoughtfully before replying.

"I think it's more like lumberjacking is not a job that requires artistry. Skill, yes. But artistry? No. The designs he makes, they're exquisite and one of a kind. Growing up the way he did, he had no chances to create beauty or art. Now that he's an adult and the master of his own life, he takes it quite seriously."

"Oh." She finished her milk and licked her lips. Now she really did want to sleep. After mind-blowing sex, warm cookies, and milk, she didn't stand a chance. She took a minute to use the restroom and brush her teeth before crawling back into bed. She heard the distant sounds of Blake doing the same after she'd snuggled beneath the covers. Who knew she'd feel so safe in Blake's bed? A moment later he got in bed beside her again.

"Sleep," Blake commanded as he leaned over her to turn off the light. Darkness blended with the moonlight coming in from the windows.

"Stop bossing me around," she grumbled, but she was smiling as she nuzzled her cheek against her pillow.

"You know you like it." He chuckled in the darkness and reached for her, tucking her into his side and laying one arm over her waist above the blankets as though they had slept like this for years.

She did like it, and him . . . and Mason. And that was a problem she would have to face tomorrow.

Chapter Four

Kisses stirred Hazel from her deep, dreamless sleep. She rolled closer to the delicious source of heat and hardness beside her. Lips moved against her neck, then up to her mouth. Hands gripped her thighs, thumbs pressed into the crease where her hips and legs met. *Yes, open me,* she silently begged as she moaned, praying for another kiss. A mouth moved against hers in a long, wonderful kiss before she felt those lips curve into a smile. She loved kisses that seemed to go on forever. A tongue teased hers, reminding her how much she missed this kind of intimacy. When the kiss stopped, she protested with a little cry. She wanted more, she wanted to be taken, to be used, to be pleasured, to be worshipped with tongues, hands, and other body parts.

"Good, you're awake," a deep voice rumbled.

It was Blake.

Oh my God . . . The memories of last night came back to her in a slow, heated wave, and her eyes flew open. She'd let Blake's friend fuck her mouth, then her pussy, all while Blake had watched approvingly. And she'd liked it . . . too much.

"Remembering what we did last night?" Blake smiled as he stroked her face. He lay beside her in his bed, his head resting on one hand as he watched her.

"Did we really . . . ?"

"Splay you open while Mason fucked you to orgasm? Oh yes, you were such a good girl, putting on that show for me." He brushed a thumb over her lower lip, and she had the distinct impression he was thinking about putting his cock between her lips. The image filled her with heat and desire. She wanted to taste him like that, to bring him to the brink of pleasurable disaster so he felt as out of control as he always made her feel.

"I've been up for two hours waiting for *my turn.*" His blue eyes were hot as he said *my turn*, and Hazel's lower belly clenched hard with responding desire. She wanted him to have his turn too.

"Where's Mason?" she asked.

"Probably making breakfast."

"Does he really like to cook?" Hazel couldn't help

but be curious about the stranger she'd given herself to last night.

"Sometimes. He cooked for his two little sisters when he was growing up. His dad died in a car accident when he was only ten, and his mother had to work two jobs to keep food in the fridge and a roof over their heads."

Hazel's chest tightened at the thought of Mason shouldering such a great responsibility at such a young age.

"And you? Do you have any siblings?" She knew a lot about Blake from his time in law school and as a lawyer, but not a lot about his past.

"No. I'm an only child. I think that's why Mason helping me that day against those bullies connected us as brothers. No one had ever stuck up for me before or defended me, but he did." Blake had always been mysterious, but to his credit, if she ever asked him a question, he answered honestly. She liked that about him. It was one of the things that made her trust him, at least enough to partially let her guard down.

"Does Mason live here with you?" she asked.

"No, he has a house on the property next to mine. Mason has different tastes in architecture and design."

"Are you two . . . in a relationship?"

He chuckled. "No, not in the way you're imagining.

We only like women, as far as those tastes run. But whenever we've lived too far apart, it's felt . . . lonely. I imagine if I had a real blood brother, I'd want to live near him too, if he was anything like Mason."

"So he didn't want to live in your posh mansion?" she teased Blake. "Let me guess, Mr. Flannel has a log cabin or something, right?"

Blake laughed. "Or something. He has a very big wooden lodge that abuts the small lake behind our two properties." Blake stroked his fingers over her cheek, then moved his hand down to her throat.

"I think you've distracted me enough for the moment," he murmured. "It's *my* turn."

He rolled her beneath him and settled between her thighs.

"Where's my shirt?" she asked as her bare breasts rubbed against his chest.

"You mean *my* shirt?" Blake arched one wicked brow at her. He lowered his lips to hers and kissed her in a way that made her toes curl.

The hardness of his shaft rubbed against her thighs, and he lifted his hips up, bracing himself with one arm while he guided himself into her. Hazel eagerly raised her hips to his, taking him deeper. She moaned as he filled her, stretched her, and she arched her back as she struggled to relax.

"Fuck . . . ," he groaned against her neck. "Are you still sore from last night?" He always seemed to know how she felt even about such intimate things.

"A little, but don't you dare stop." She dug her nails into his buttocks.

"Bossy little thing, aren't you?" He laughed and surged into her again.

"You know you like it," she tried to argue, but he hit a spot deep inside her that made her squeak, and her eyes blurred with wonderful stars. She hooked her legs around his narrow, powerful hips and groaned. She was still sore from Mason fucking her hard last night, but as she clenched around Blake's cock, she didn't care. The friction of their skin, the feel of her body tightening, and the sensation of spinning wildly in a thousand directions was almost too much.

He made love to her slowly, deeply, covering her with kisses and murmuring soft, sweet things in her ears that filled her head with visions of what could be between them. As she came in a slow, burning, beautiful orgasm, she still continued to hunger for him . . . Or so it always seemed. She began to come down from the glorious high, and as she became more relaxed beneath him, he fucked her harder, deeper, his lips curved in a dark smile. He took his pleasure and called her his good little girl in a way that made her whimper and clamp down even tighter around his cock. How could he make her feel so desired, so lusted after, and bring her to the brink of sexual madness all with just the way he moved inside and on top of her?

"Is that all you've got, London?" she challenged him, and he collapsed on top of her. She embraced his waist, loving how he pinned her to the bed without crushing her.

Blake shot her a scorching look. "Not even close." He withdrew from her and sat up on the edge of the bed. Then he opened the bedside drawer and pulled out two leather cuffs lined with fleece. Blake chuckled between hard breaths. "I've missed you, Hazel. God, how I've missed you."

"Giving up?" she teased.

"I think turnabout is fair play."

Her gaze dropped to the cuffs in his hands, and the sight made her nipples harden into buds and her skin blaze with a wave of heat. He knew just what she wanted, what she needed from him.

He captured her wrists and stretched her arms above her head, hooking the cuffs onto a metal chain that he'd hidden between the mattress and the headboard. He lifted one end of the chain to secure it on a small hook at the top of the headboard, keeping her hands close together.

Hazel's heart began to pound as he pulled the covers of the bed back to expose her naked body. She clamped her thighs together, hoping to hide her slickness from her previous orgasm as he stared at her. His gaze dropped to her legs, and his lips twitched in a half smirk, as if he knew what she was trying to do.

"For the next week, you are my toy, Hazel. *Mine.* I think it's time you learned what that means." Blake removed a small vibrator from a drawer in the dresser and came back over to the bed. She opened her legs, waiting eagerly for him to slide it into her wet, aching core, but Blake shook his head, amused.

"Oh no, little one. You aren't getting away from your punishment for teasing me about my stamina that easily." He rolled her onto her stomach, and she heard him open a tube of lube. She gasped as he parted her ass cheeks and pressed the cold, wet tip of the vibrator against her anus. It pushed against the tight ring of muscle, stretching her as he pushed it inside.

"Blake . . . oh God . . ." She gasped at the feel of the foreign object inside her. Suddenly, it began to vibrate. She nearly shrieked in shock. Blake gently rolled her onto her back again and leaned over her, holding up a small black remote for her to see.

"I think half an hour of using this will remind you that when you're in my bed, *you're mine* to play with."

The vibrations increased in intensity as she lay there with her wrists still cuffed above her head. Blake set the remote out of reach and lowered his head to her throat, kissing her. She tilted her head back, letting him move his lips wherever he wished because it felt so good. If he dared to move lower, she would come, she was sure of it . . .

He stroked fingers along her rib cage, over her belly, circling, then pressing down, and gripping hard, never repeating one gesture long enough for her to focus on it and let her climax build. She growled in frustration and tried to move her body to get his hand where she wanted it, but he removed his hand.

Her thighs squeezed tightly as her channel ached to take him. She *needed* to come. She felt it building, that exquisite pleasure she craved, but all of a sudden, the vibrations in her ass ceased, and Blake lifted his head from her neck with a grin. He slid off the bed and gave her a long, scorching look. He then retrieved some clothing and disappeared into his bathroom.

Hazel cursed softly as the orgasm that had been so close faded away, and she was left unsatisfied. A few minutes later, Blake emerged from the bathroom wearing jeans and a T-shirt. He picked up a large three-ring binder from his dresser, along with a pen and a pad of sticky notes. Blake settled back in bed beside her and opened the binder in his lap. From where she lay, she could see the pages he was examining.

"You're looking at prebills right now?" she asked. "Are you kidding me?" She wriggled against the restraints. How the hell could he want to look at prebills for clients when she needed to come?

Oh . . . that was his evil plan. To tease her and keep her from coming. Damn, the man was too clever. It would be torture to get close to the edge of an orgasm and not be able to climax. She shouldn't have teased him about giving up after just one climax.

He chuckled as if he could read her thoughts and turned another page of his prebills. He made a note on one of the client invoices and turned yet another page. His dark hair fell into his eyes, and he brushed it away with his elegant but strong fingers. Fingers that she wished were inside her, touching her.

"You play dirty," she accused softly.

He glanced down at her. "You like me because I'm not a saint."

"You're more like a comic book villain," she added thoughtfully.

"I don't think Lex Luthor ever tied up Superman and used sex toys on him," Blake replied. "But you know what? I rather like being your kryptonite, Hazel. Perhaps while I have your attention, we can discuss the upcoming sale of the Reynolds Corporation between your client and mine."

Business. Now he was talking business, the cad. *The sexy as hell cad,* she silently amended. He picked up the remote from the table and brushed his thumb over the red button.

So Blake wanted to play? She could beat him at this game, she was certain of it. She had before, hadn't she?

"Fine, you want to talk business? As the owners of the Reynolds Corporation, my clients will demand at least a 40 percent bonus for the higher-level employees they retain after the sale." She knew what he was going to argue next.

"Ten percent bonuses," he countered, and pressed the button.

She jolted when the vibrations started again, and she tried and failed to hide a moan as she clenched her thighs together. She arched her back, attempting to get him to notice her bare breasts. He'd had a fondness for them in the past. His heated gaze settled on her breasts, and he set his prebills binder aside so he could trail a finger around one of her nipples. It tightened into a stiff peak at his touch.

"Lady Godiva rode into battle bare-breasted, just like you," he murmured.

"Well, she knew that men are easily distracted,"

Hazel replied, her tone breathless as he lightly pinched her nipple. He was the one distracting her, and they both knew it. The pulsing from the vibrator increased, and she could feel her body priming for another climax.

Blake leaned his head down to her breast, taking her nipple into his mouth and sucking on it in a way that sent electric bolts of pleasure through her. Yes, she was going to come, she—

He lifted his head, and the vibrations immediately ceased. She hissed out a frustrated breath.

"Ten percent," he said, and continued to watch her. He knew that she wasn't good at coming on her own. She'd never been able to do what some other women seemed to do so easily. They could just touch themselves and come. She'd always needed a touch that wasn't her own.

"Forty percent," she countered. She wasn't going to back down, no matter how much she wanted to come.

They battled for another twenty minutes, him bringing her right to the edge and then backing off, over and over. Her body was covered in sweat and so needy to come that she was shaking. A plea of surrender to him on every level hung on her lips, an instant away from being uttered. He made it so hard to resist him when he knew just how to torture her with pleasure.

Before she could speak, the bedroom door opened,

and Mason walked inside. He wore faded blue jeans and a green henley, the sleeves pulled up to his elbows to expose bronzed forearms. He looked like walking sin, and she wanted a taste of him.

"Ah, I was wondering why no one turned up for breakfast. It's ready."

"Mason." She exhaled in relief. He would give her what she needed.

"Morning, sweetheart," he greeted with a warm smile, as if they were meeting for coffee and not like she was cuffed to a bed naked in front of him and begging Blake for a climax.

"I need you," she told Mason and parted her legs, lifting her hips suggestively in a clear invitation. He wouldn't leave her like this.

"You certainly do," he agreed, his voice deepening a little. "But I see that Blake is in the middle of something."

"Our pet needed a reminder that she is ours, Mason, ours to play with," Blake replied as if talking about the weather.

Mason grinned. "Let me guess, she got bossy with you, didn't she?"

"I don't mind when she's bossy, but she dared to challenge my stamina, and I couldn't allow that."

"Oh, Hazel, sweetheart." Mason sighed dramatically. "You shouldn't have done that."

Hazel narrowed her eyes at Mason. "Traitor," she accused.

Unfazed by her remark, he leaned against the dresser and crossed his arms, not coming any closer. "As much as I'm enjoying this, breakfast will get cold, Blake."

"Oh, all right." Blake sighed, closed his prebill binder, and set it aside. "Care to watch?" he asked his friend.

"Absolutely." Mason made a show of settling in. His eyes seemed to drink in the sight of her like a thirsty man eyeing a pitcher of cold water.

Blake flipped her onto her stomach and urged her to her knees. She had enough loose chain attached to her cuffs to be able to brace her palms on the middle of the headboard. Blake knelt behind her, and she smiled triumphantly as she heard him unzip his jeans. Now she was going to get what she wanted. But her smile died as the vibrations started in her ass again. He wasn't going to take it out? She'd never had two things penetrate her at the same time.

"Blake, I . . ." She inhaled sharply as he thrust into her wet folds and his cock rubbed intimately against the vibrator in her ass. The double penetration was . . . *amazing.*

"You have to be prepared if you're going to take both of us at the same time," Blake whispered in her ear before he bit the lobe and thrust even deeper into her. "One of us will be here, deep inside your tight wet heat, and the other will be in that delectable ass of yours."

Hazel cried out at the picture his words painted, her body almost in pain as she held on to the headboard. The climax that exploded through her was as fierce as a forest fire and just as devastating, but she embraced it completely.

Blake fisted a hand in her hair and pulled a little, making her tilt her head back. Mason watched, silent, his gaze one of raw lust as Blake began a merciless and fast-paced taking of her body. One of Blake's hands roved over her breasts and down to her clit, feathering light touches before sliding back up to cup a breast again. He pumped his hips, surging deep into her, over and over, filling her until she gasped from the sudden pressure of his entry.

This time he whispered hot, deliciously dirty things in her ear about what he wanted to do to her, how he wanted to stretch her, make her his sweet little girl who would crawl on her knees to him and suck him off. He wanted to spank her ass until it was red while she came apart on Mason's cock . . . So many wicked things spilled from his sinfully full lips. And all the while, he pounded into her from behind, never relenting.

He moved so fast that her body couldn't adjust to his rhythm or move with him. He was using her like a toy, just as he'd promised he would, and when she realized that, she came hard a second time, her throat raw from a scream of pure, blinding pleasure that made her close her eyes.

She clawed at the headboard, and when her eyes opened again, she saw Mason still staring at her. A tic worked in his jaw and the muscles of his arms flexed as though he was fighting the need to come to her. The only thing she wanted in that moment was for Mason to be there in bed with her and Blake. She craved to be overwhelmed by them. She wanted them to make her forget every worry she had.

Blake panted against her neck, his fist still in her hair as his harsh breaths warmed her sweat-dewed skin. His cock was buried deep inside her, and the vibrations in her ass rumbled through her body, drawing out little jerking aftershocks that made her twitch around Blake's cock. He moaned, rocking his hips against her ass, sliding in and out of Hazel a little, even though her inner walls attempted to hold him inside.

"All right, 40 percent," he whispered. "I'll give you forty."

He kissed her throat and held her in a tight, all-encompassing hug. Their bodies were still intimately joined, and somehow that intensified the moment and their embrace. She caught her breath, sagging back against him, and closed her eyes again. To be held by Blake was something truly exquisite. Especially like this. How had she forgotten how safe his arms made her feel?

Someone undid the cuffs on her wrists, and she knew it had to be Mason because Blake still had one hand in her hair and one hand along her breast, playing with her nipple and kneading gently.

"I knew you would see things my way," she told Blake between her own heavy breaths.

Mason laughed hard. "You've got your hands full with this one, don't you?" he said to Blake before meeting her gaze again. "Hazel, sweetheart, take a quick shower, then join me for breakfast." Mason was still laughing as he walked out of the bedroom.

Blake continued to hold her for a long moment before he finally turned the vibrator off and pulled it out of her body.

"You may have won our negotiation, but I won *this*," he murmured huskily against her mouth as he slid three of his fingers into the wet heat between her thighs.

She couldn't disagree with that. He had triumphed in bed . . . Well, she had too, if one counted the number of her orgasms. He pressed a soft, open-mouthed kiss to her lips before climbing off the bed and disappearing into the bathroom. She was still sitting on the edge of the bed, her legs too shaky to stand, when he returned to the bedroom.

"Can you walk?" he asked, half-teasing, half-serious.

"Yes." It wasn't quite a lie.

"I'll go downstairs and see what Mason's fixed for us."

She waited for Blake to leave the bedroom before she walked to the bathroom. Her body still hummed, even though she no longer had the vibrator or Blake inside her. She was going to be feeling him and that vibrator for a few hours, but she wasn't complaining. Once more she was glad to have some space to think. Blake had a way of muddling her thoughts.

She admired the black granite countertops and the gold hardware of the handles and faucets. It was tasteful and not overdone. She stepped into the shower and turned it on. Water blasted at her from different angles, and she sighed luxuriously as the hot water covered her skin. She wanted to linger and take a sinfully long shower, but knowing Mason had cooked breakfast downstairs hurried her along. She used Blake's expensive shampoo, conditioner, and body wash, and couldn't help but smile as she inhaled the scent that smelled just like Blake. It was a soft scent, with a hint of pine and amber.

She dried off and used a hairdryer that Blake had left on the counter for her. When she finished, she rummaged around Blake's dresser in the bedroom and stole a pair of his boxers and the white dress shirt he'd worn last night. It still smelled like him, and she rubbed her cheek against one sleeve before she rolled up the cuffs. While she liked tiptoeing around in Blake's clothing, she knew at some point she was going to have to convince Mason or Blake to go to her apartment in the city and bring her some of her own clothes.

Hazel followed her nose downstairs to the kitchen to find Mason and Blake both huddled around the island, softly talking to each other and drinking coffee.

"You hungry?" Mason asked when they spotted her. Together they looked more like brothers, as they both wore jeans. She was more used to seeing Blake in his bespoke business suits, which she adored, but getting a glimpse of his relaxed side made her heart flutter traitorously. It reminded her too much of law school and that night they'd shared. She wanted to go to him and hug him and bury her face against his chest, just to feel safe and cherished. And that was something she couldn't let herself do. She needed to limit it to amazing sex with him and Mason. Nothing more.

"What's on the menu?" she asked them and pasted a smile on her face to hide her thoughts.

"*You* . . . later, of course," Mason said with a chuckle. "Right now, there are pancakes, eggs, bacon, coffee, and tea. What sounds good to you?"

"I want all of that except the coffee. I would love a cup of Earl Grey tea, black, if you have it?"

"You got it, sweetheart. Have a seat." Mason nodded at the cozy table where someone, probably Chalmers, had set up for breakfast.

She glanced at Blake when she saw only two place settings.

"Enjoy breakfast," Blake murmured and winked at her. "I have to call my client to break the bad news about the bonuses on the Reynolds Corporation sale."

So it was just going to be her and Mason? Hazel took a seat and tried to quell the slight flutter of nerves as she watched Mason load up a plate of food and steep a cup of tea for her. He and Blake had fucked the hell out of her, but damned if they didn't treat her like a princess too. It was something else she couldn't get used to. She'd lost her parents in college—one to cancer, the other to a stroke a year later—and she'd gotten used to taking care of herself pretty quickly. It wasn't easy to let go of the habit of relying only on herself.

"Thank you," she replied as he set the food down in front of her and gave her the cup of tea.

"Warm syrup?" he asked as he placed a small carafe next to her plate.

"You really go all out," she noted as she poured syrup on her pancakes. But she instantly regretted her words when Mason's brown eyes darkened with shadows of old pain.

"I liked cooking a big breakfast for my little sisters and my mother on Sunday mornings. It was the only day my mother had off for the entire week. She would be utterly exhausted, so I would let her sleep in and cook for her and my sisters. It felt like one of the few nice things I could do between the housework and yardwork."

Damn, the man had a way of making her want to cuddle up in his lap and purr. It was such a sweet thing to do for his family.

"Is your mother still alive?" she asked, hoping her question wasn't too insensitive.

"Yes. She's retired now. The moment my business took off, I made sure that I could support her. She has a house in Palm Springs and doesn't ever have to work again. Of course, she's not used to so much leisure time, so she runs a charity now. She could never stay still for long, but at least her hours are her own choosing, and she doesn't have to answer to anyone ever again."

Hazel remembered what Blake had told her about Mason's father. "I imagine your father would be proud of you."

Mason paused in the act of pouring himself more coffee. "I would like to think he would be too. What about you? Any siblings?"

"No," she replied, feeling suddenly subdued. She didn't like talking about her past. It hurt, but he had shared some of himself with her, and it felt wrong to close up to him.

"I was an only child. I was a freshman in college when my mother died from breast cancer. My dad was gone a year later from a stroke. He was so healthy, the doctors couldn't believe he'd died like that. Part of me—" She halted as a lump formed in her throat.

Mason sat down in the chair beside her and covered her hand with his. "You don't have to tell me anything."

Oh, but she did. These were things Blake knew about her, and she wanted Mason to know them too, even if it hurt to say them. Mason didn't push her, though, and let her take her time to speak.

"It probably sounds silly, but secretly, I think he died of a broken heart. He and my mom were soulmates.

I think the doctors just didn't know what to put down on his death certificate."

Mason's jaw clenched briefly before he relaxed. "I hate that you lost them. It's a crime to lose a parent so young, and you lost both of yours."

Tears suddenly sprang from her eyes. God, she hated crying, yet here she was blubbering like an idiot.

"You lost your dad far younger than I did," she tried to argue.

He leaned over and cupped her face in his hand. "Don't cry, sweetheart. Those tears will wreck me forever." He kissed her, his mouth soft and sweet, and the tears came harder as she abandoned her seat and lunged for him. He pushed his chair back and pulled her onto his lap, cradling her against his chest. He kissed her again, and like before, it was not a kiss to seduce. It was a kiss to soothe away her pain and console her. It was a kiss that held an infinite sense of something that she feared and craved all at once. It was a kiss full of love. How could that be possible? She hadn't known him for even a full day, and yet something was growing between her and this gorgeous man. She buried her face in his shirt and fought off more tears.

"Let it out, sweetheart. These are tears that you need to shed, even if it kills me to see you cry. Someone once told me that to heal you must *feel*." His kindness made it worse, and she felt even more wretched.

"Either the pancakes were very good or very bad . . . ," Blake said from behind them.

Hazel frantically rubbed her eyes to erase the evidence of her tears before she dared to meet Blake's searching gaze.

"I didn't even get to try them," she muttered from Mason's lap.

"No, you don't get to run when you're hurting," Mason said firmly, even though his tone was gentle.

"He's right. I know you like your space," Blake added as he joined them at the table, "but when you're hurting and need comfort? That's when you need one or both of us to care for you."

"I can take care of myself. I always have."

"We're saying you don't have to," Blake replied. "Right, Mason?"

"Right." Mason reached for her plate and poured a little extra syrup over her pancakes. "I'm going to feed you these pancakes, and you are going to let me."

"Am I?" She tried to sound argumentative, but it came out more like a tremulous question.

"Yes, because your tears hurt me, sweetheart. Holding you and feeding you will make me feel better right now."

"It's best not to argue with Mason," Blake said with a soft smile. "He's usually right."

Hazel felt silly letting a man feed her, but there was something sweet about it and also a little arousing. Blake took a chair opposite her and Mason and watched them, his gaze impossibly soft. When she couldn't eat another bite, Mason patted her waist.

"You up for visiting my place for a little while?"

"Your place?" she echoed, suddenly remember that he'd said his home was nearby.

"I'd like to show you."

She shot a glance at Blake as he sipped his coffee. He merely smiled and said nothing.

"Okay." She'd barely finished the word when Mason stood and cradled her in his arms.

"Oh!" She clutched at his neck in fear of being dropped. "Put me down. I can walk."

"If Blake did his job properly this morning, you should be glad to have me carry you. Besides, I like holding you. You can't run away when I do." He grinned at her and headed for the large glass doors at the back of the kitchen that faced the lake.

Mason's home. She was going to see where this mysterious man lived. A little thrill shot through her, but she tamped it down. Six more days. All she had to do was not fall in love in the next six days. She could manage that, right?

Chapter Five

Mason carried his prize in his arms as he crossed the perfectly manicured lawn belonging to Blake and passed into a garden of wildflowers and homegrown vegetables. Beyond the garden he saw his home, the rough-hewn timber lodge with a large secondary building behind it that housed his carpentry workshop. She shifted in his arms, her gaze taking in the world around them, and he tried to see his home through Hazel's eyes.

The last week's storm clouds hadn't completely vanished from the horizon. All around them everything was a vibrant green. That was his favorite color. Green was life, it was beauty, it was everything that gave a person hope that all would be well after a storm. Hazel's eyes held beautiful flecks of green mixed with brown, and he loved that green the best. He wondered if Hazel liked green as much as he did.

Light dappled him and Hazel as they walked beneath the shelter of the ginkgo trees that surrounded his estate. It had taken years to grow them to a decent height, but their leaves in the fall would cover the grass with a blanket of pure gold. Hazel silently studied her surroundings, and Mason would have given anything to hear her thoughts. Did she like the way he'd structured his gardens and the woods around the house, creating a wildness blended with planned beauty?

He climbed the steps of his porch and set her down on her feet. She wore no shoes, but he didn't worry. He had sanded and polished this deck himself. It was utterly smooth. Mason opened the door and gestured for her to go inside. She went ahead of him, and he stared at the tumble of reddish-auburn hair that trailed down her back. His hand flexed as he resisted the urge to grab her hair and use it to spin her into his arms to steal a kiss. That would of course lead to a lot more than a kiss, and he wanted to show her that what he wanted with her wasn't just sex. She rubbed her arms and glanced around his home before turning back to him as he closed the door.

"It's so beautiful. It's warm and cozy, even though it's big," she replied.

"You like it?"

She nodded, a delicate blush blossoming on her cheeks. His heart stuttered. He'd already had her in his arms and in a bed, but this . . . having her in his home? It touched something deep within him, like she'd cast a stone upon the still lake of his soul and now he was feeling the ripples of her presence. Mason rarely let anyone into his home. It was his private sanctuary. He'd never brought any woman here before. He hadn't dated anyone seriously in his life. He had spent nights with women in expensive hotel rooms, or at their homes, but he was always gone the next day. This was different. Because this was *Hazel*. How many times had Blake told him about this woman while they'd shared beers and fished on their lake, or while they'd quietly sipped whiskeys while talking about a particularly long week of work?

Hazel was always on his best friend's mind, and now she was burned into Mason's soul. Perhaps he should be afraid, should run, but he always listened to his heart rather than his head, and his heart beat a steady rhythm to this woman's name.

Hazel. Hazel. Hazel.

"Where do you work?" Hazel asked as she turned her back on him to look around at the room.

Mason's gaze strayed to her ass, and he admired openly how cute she looked in Blake's dress shirt and boxers.

"Follow me." Mason led her through the house and into a glassed-in walkway he'd built that connected the workshop and his lodge. He unlocked the door to the workshop and went in first, hitting the light switch. The main floor was three thousand square feet, and dozens of Edison lights illuminated the various projects he was working on. There was a beautiful four-poster bed for a fashion heiress living in Milan, a dresser for a famous architect from Seattle, two matching desks for a married couple who ran their own business and had recently invested in some private Caribbean resorts, and a boat for a client in Maine who liked to sail. The last project he was currently working on was a cradle. Hazel moved through the warehouse, admiring each piece and asking him questions.

"How did you discover you liked working with wood?" she asked when they reached the dresser.

"It's kind of a silly story," he said as he rubbed the back of his neck, heat filling his face.

"Then tell me. The best stories are always a little bit

silly." She said this with a serious face, but mischief glinted in her eyes and put him at ease.

"My sisters had a dresser; it was an old wood thing my mom purchased at a neighbor's garage sale. We didn't have much room in our trailer, but we did have a space for something to put the girls' clothes in. Well, the bottom drawer always got stuck. It had warped over time from exposure to humidity, which wasn't unusual." He remembered all too easily—the frustrating summer days when he'd knelt in front of that dresser, his little sisters clustered around him waiting for him to wiggle the drawer free so they could find T-shirts or shorts. How he'd hated that dresser and all the grief it caused him until he figured out how to fix it. He'd tugged and tugged and almost broken the drawer, and his eye had twitched for weeks whenever he'd looked at the damned thing.

"A lot of people don't use the AC in the summer if they can survive without it to save money. That stuck drawer drove us all crazy. One afternoon, I went to my school's computer lab and researched online what to do if drawers were stuck like that. I found a bunch of tutorials about using sandpaper and oil. I used my meager savings from my after-school job to buy supplies to fix the drawer. That made me feel like a hero, to walk into that hardware store and buy what I needed to fix the drawer. It was the first time I felt capable of fixing something, and I've been chasing that feeling of fixing things and building things ever since. After I bought sandpaper and oil, I wedged the drawer out, sanded the warped areas, and oiled the whole thing up. Most dressers have metal sliders that are pre-oiled now, but this one was so old that it was made entirely of wood." Feeling that smooth, sanded drawer beneath his palm when he'd followed the training instructions he'd found online had changed him. He'd made something broken work again. And something that he hadn't realized had been broken within him suddenly felt . . . mended.

"Wait, how old were you when this happened?" she asked.

"Twelve." Mason knew what she would say next. She was a lawyer, and a good one at that.

"But you couldn't work legally at twelve."

"But I did . . . sort of. I helped out a neighbor who was on disability. He paid me in cash for chores like lawn mowing and helping around the house. Obviously, only my mom knew about the work I was doing. We needed the money."

"Oh." Hazel's eyes softened, not with pity but compassion, and he saw the flecks of green in her eyes deepen.

"Can you show me how to sand something?" she asked curiously as she stroked the edge of the desk they were standing next to with her slender fingers.

Mason took her hand in his, examining her fingers, and smiled. "I would be happy to." Then he brushed his lips over her knuckles. He didn't let go of her hand. It felt too good, too natural to hold her hand with his own. He led her toward the cradle. It was a sturdy design, elegantly carved with wild animals like deer, rabbits, and badgers as well as foxes, to give it a sort of woodland fairy-tale look to it. He wasn't yet finished sanding the spindle, so he retrieved a piece of sandpaper from a packet nearby, wrapped it around the spindle, and gently moved the paper up and down, grinding it against the wood.

"Do it like that. You try." He gave her a piece of her own sandpaper and reluctantly released her other hand. She mimicked what he had shown her, moving her hands with gentle motions but hard enough to sand the entire spindle.

"You'll know when it's finished because it's smooth to your touch."

She sanded for a minute or two in silence, her expression one of deep concentration.

"Do you . . . do you want children?" she asked.

"Kids?" The single word held a universe of questions as he spoke it.

"Yeah." She didn't look at him as she ran her fingers along the spindle, testing its smoothness.

"I do, but I'm not sure I'll ever have them," he said, watching her face closely to see her reaction.

"Why not?" She finally met his eyes.

Heat climbed his cheeks, not because he was embarrassed, but because he wasn't used to talking about his deepest desires this openly. "Because any woman I would want that life with? I would want to share her with Blake. And that's a complicated request for us to make of a woman."

"Does Blake want children?" she asked, another blush betraying her.

"Yes." He gave a breathy chuckle. "He feels the same about it as I do. We are a package deal. We want to share one woman between us."

"That is complicated," Hazel agreed. "But surely someone out there would agree to that, if they loved you both."

Mason didn't say anything more as she picked up a second piece of sandpaper and handed it to him. They sanded the cradle together for several long minutes in silence.

"So, Mr. Boy Scout, are you an expert on knots?" Hazel asked.

"Knots?" He brushed away dust from the spindles and set his sandpaper down.

"You know . . . to tie things up?" She gave him a meaningful look.

"Tie things up or tie *you* up?" Mason asked with a grin as he caught on to her game.

"I'll give you one guess which," she said, and Mason didn't hesitate.

He snatched her up in his arms and threw her over his shoulder. He gripped the back of her legs with one arm and rested his other hand on her ass, giving it a light, possessive smack. She laughed and then shrieked as he carried her through the warehouse toward the sailboat. It was a small boat, and he'd turned it upside down to work on the hull, leaving the bottom of the vessel the perfect height to put a woman on top of. Hazel wriggled as he set her down on it, and he reached for a coil of nearby rope. It was a smooth rope of braided cotton, and as long as she didn't tug on the knots too much, he guessed it wouldn't hurt her wrists.

He wound the white rope around her wrists in a two-half hitch knot that could easily be undone with a tug on the right spot. Then he stretched her hands above her head and secured the other end of the rope to the opposite end of the boat, leaving her flat on her back on the newly waxed surface of the hull.

Hazel stared up at him as he leaned over her, grinning.

"My scoutmaster would be proud—that is one hell of a double hitch knot," he said, nodding at her hands above her head. He pulled something out of his pocket, and her eyes widened and then narrowed at him.

This was going to be fun.

He had gagged her.

Mason had tied a strip of cloth around her head and put it between her lips. She could still easily scream, still make sounds, but just not talk clearly.

He leaned in close and toyed with the edge of the gag by her cheek. "If you're wondering why I like this, it's because I like hearing your muffled voice," he whispered. "It reminds me of the fact that I caught you, little rabbit, and I'm going to fuck you right here."

Oh God, he *knew*, they both knew, that she liked being chased and fucked. It was her deepest, darkest fantasy. Had Blake told him?

He stroked a fingertip down her chin to her throat and then along her collarbone.

"That's a nice shirt, but Blake can afford to buy a new one." He curled his fingers in the cloth and tore at it.

Buttons flew everywhere as Mason peeled the dress shirt open, baring her breasts to him. He stared at her a long moment, his eyes glowing with desire.

Hazel breathed hard as her own lust went into overdrive.

He bent his head and sucked one of her nipples into his mouth. Her body arched off the smooth hull, the pull at the flesh of her breast zinging straight to her pussy. She moaned around the gag and tried to breathe as his other hand slid under the elastic of her boxers to cup her mound. She strained against the ropes, her muscles pulling, her thighs parting to give him better access. His fingers stroked her labia and abruptly stopped and smacked the delicate flesh up near her clit. She squeaked as his head jerked free of her nipple, leaving it shiny and cold in the air of the workshop.

"Naughty girl." His growl was low, but the light in his eyes promised she would like being called that as much as she liked being Blake's *good girl*.

She whimpered as his fingers stroked along her pussy again, rubbing through the wetness of the folds and teasing her. Her bare feet tried to find purchase on the floor, and she widened her legs and angled upward to wrap her legs around him, but he stepped back.

She grunted in frustration, and he chuckled. "Such a naughty girl."

She started to aim a glare at him but lost her mind when he hooked his fingers in the waistband of the boxers and pulled them off her legs. Before she could process her own nakedness, he lifted her legs and spread them around his hips, her wet core pressed against the roughness of the zipper of his jeans. Her nipples pebbled into hard points and her stomach tightened in anticipation as she waited for him to do what he would with her prone, primed body.

He leaned over her, his heat tingling her skin, and licked his lips. "Good girls get eaten out. But naughty girls . . ."

She squirmed as he dragged his eyes down her body, keenly aware of the hardness that pushed against his fly, nestled between her legs. She scooted forward slightly to better feel his cock, and he chuckled.

"Naughty girl, then. In that case . . ." He lifted her body a little and gently rolled her over so that she lay face down on the smoothly waxed hull of the boat.

Smack! His palm lightly connected with her buttocks as he spanked her. The smack hurt, but it sent a flood of desire following straight afterward. The heat of his palm, the way he jerked her body, moving it where he wanted so he could punish her better, only melted her inside that much quicker. Something dark and secretly wicked within her liked being spanked, liked being punished like this for teasing him and Blake. She loved pushing against their boundaries and still being safe, even if she got spanked for it.

"Ten ought to do it," he said, then he gave her nine more spankings, each a little harder. By the end she was hot all over and dripping for him.

When he turned her back over to face him, he once more bent his head to her breasts, nuzzling them before nipping at a sensitive peak. She let out a cry through the gag as pleasure zinged straight to her core. The ropes pulled against her wrists as she struggled, but she didn't mind. She could handle a little bruising, especially if she had done it herself in her own excitement. Her body quivered as she arched her back, offering more of herself to Mason. He groaned and buried his face in the valley of her breasts as he drew in a deep breath.

"You are the only woman I've ever met who makes me lose control. I've taken women to bed before and have never felt so mindless as I do now." He lifted his head to look up at her. "*You* do this to me, Hazel. *Only you.*" He kissed his way down to her mound. Before, he had handled her roughly, but this time his lips and mouth were sensitive and gentle. He licked and kissed slowly, taking his time tasting her. Each flick of his tongue on her tender, sensitive flesh was too much. She was grateful for the gag because knowing her cries were muffled allowed her to be as loud as she desired. Mason's tongue circled the bud of her clit before he drew it between his lips. She jerked tighter against the soft cotton ropes that held her prisoner.

"Beg for me, sweetheart," Mason growled as he reached up to tease the gag out of her mouth.

She sucked in a deep breath, about to say she would never beg a man for anything, but when he looked at her with those burning brown eyes, darkened with sensual secrets, she found herself surrendering.

"Please, Mason," she begged.

"Please, *sir*," he corrected. "If you want gentle love-making, you call me *Mason*, and I'll give you what you want. But if you want me to wreck you, you'll call me *sir*, understand?" He slid one finger inside her, pumping lightly to remind her of what she *really* wanted.

"Please . . . sir." She lifted her hips, and Mason's face lit with a wicked smile.

"As you wish, sweetheart." He unfastened his jeans, freed his cock, and within seconds he was thrusting deep, so hard that she cried out at the sudden pressure. He leaned over her, bracing his hands on the boat before he suddenly caught her hands and held them. Even though she was still tied up, his fingers curled around her wrists. Trapping her only heightened the feeling of helplessness in this situation, and she loved it. He moved his other hand to grasp her hip, holding her steady as he withdrew and drove deep again. They both gasped at the same time as he filled her and stretched her.

"So goddamn tight," he murmured against her parted lips, kissing her. It was one of the best kisses of her life. She let go of all thoughts, all fears, all worries. There was nothing beyond this kiss and the motion of their bodies joining. She felt an ancient rhythm of two hearts and two bodies coming together as one. This was a man she could love—*was loving* in this moment—and that realization made her tremble and quake. She was losing the battle to guard her heart. Mason had just crumbled the walls of her fortress with one well-placed cannon shot.

Mason deepened the kiss, his mouth urgent on hers. He kissed her as if this might be the last time he would ever kiss her, and she returned it, tears stinging her eyes as her body began to fly. Sharp, almost painful pleasure ripped through her with the force of a tidal wave, drawing water back across the sands of her existence and pulling her out into the deep dark sea where she had no control anymore. She rocked on that ocean,

Mason with her, his heat and his strength surrounding her like the rays of the late-summer sun. He kissed away her tears, murmured soft, sweet things to her, things she needed to believe, because if she didn't, she would lose herself to the fears and anxiety outside him and this moment.

Mason brushed his lips over her cheek and drew a shaky breath against her skin.

"Blake may let you go, but not me, Hazel. I keep what's *mine*. I love it and cherish it, and once it's mine, it's mine *forever*." He lifted his face a little so their eyes could meet. He was still buried deep in her body, and yet despite his claim that she was his, she knew she was the one who could own him. All she had to do was take one step across the line and let her heart be open again. And that was terrifying.

Mason's nose nuzzled hers before he gave her one more slow, tender kiss that was no less seductive than the ones that had come before. But this one held his heart in it. All she had to do was take it . . . if she was brave enough.

When he finally withdrew from her body and fixed his clothes, she missed the feel of being joined with him. He pulled on one end of the knotted ropes that bound her, and the bindings came loose. Then he removed the rope and lightly rubbed her wrists, examining them.

There were faint red marks from her pulling, but she didn't mind. His brows lowered and he frowned.

"It doesn't hurt," she said. "I like it a little rough with marks." She thought of the marks left from Blake's ring on her hip, when he'd gripped her hips tight while making love to her. She wasn't exactly a masochist, but she did like the occasional proof of mind-blowing sex.

Mason pressed his lips to her skin in a reverent kiss before he helped her off the boat and lifted her up in his arms. He carried her back to his home and brought her straight to his bedroom. In some ways it was a lot like Blake's, spacious and well decorated, but the style was vastly different. Where Blake's room was subtle in tone and modern, Mason's room fit with his love of the outdoors. A green-and-blue plaid coverlet lay across the sleigh bed, and moss-green walls created an earthy feel. Photographs of mountains and birch tree forests in large frames decorated the space.

Mason opened the closet door and pulled out a red-and-gray plaid flannel shirt. "Put this on."

Then he gave her a fresh pair of boxers and showed her to the bathroom.

He left her alone for a few minutes to see to her needs, and when she emerged from the bathroom, he was waiting for her. Unlike Blake, who'd given her space, Mason simply leaned back against the bed and opened his arms. She went willingly to him. He held her tight, his arms banded around her and his lips buried in the crown of her hair.

"Don't be afraid of *this* . . . of me," he murmured.

She wasn't afraid of *him*, but rather of love. People who loved you could leave you, they could die, and what if something happened to him or Blake? How could she ever bear to lose one or both of them?

What if . . .

Those two words held a universe of possible heartbreak. It was so much safer to be alone, but what he and Blake promised her was too wonderful to resist for long. What would she choose when her seven days were up?

* * *

Blake watched the scene unfolding on his laptop. The security cameras in Mason's workshop had notified him of movement. He hadn't been surprised to see Hazel on her back, Mason between her thighs, fucking her hard. Blake wished he could be there, touching her, kissing her, but she needed to be alone with Mason, to learn about him and make up her mind about whether she wanted to be with him. Blake would have his own chance to convince her soon.

He curled his fingers and uncurled them, flexing his

hands on his thighs as he considered what he would do to win Hazel's love. Because the truth was, neither Mason nor he would allow her to leave when the week was over. So he had to find a way to show her she wanted them, both of them, *forever*.

As Mason carried Hazel in his arms and walked out of the frame, Blake slowly closed his laptop and steepled his fingers, staring into the distance and contemplating his next move in his seduction of Hazel Callahan.

Chapter Six

Hazel wandered back to Blake's house on her own that evening and searched room by room until she found him in his office. It was a beautifully masculine space that fit him perfectly. Something about this room and the way it carried his personality sent a sensual awareness fluttering beneath her skin. Blake was seated at his desk, typing something on his laptop. His gaze lifted to hers as she paused in the doorway.

"Ah, I wondered when you'd come back to me." He said this softly, his gaze slowly roving over her body, and she knew he could see she was wearing Mason's flannel shirt and boxers. Would he guess what they'd done in the workshop? A flush crept up her neck to her face. The way he'd said *come back to me* warmed something deep inside her chest that she hadn't realized had felt frozen. She'd wanted to come back to him, to feel his arms around her, to kiss him, to just be near him. And damned if that didn't scare the hell out of her.

"Chalmers just dropped off some clothing for you, as well as this." Blake placed a hand on her slender platinum laptop that sat on his desk. "I thought you might want to keep tabs on any pending work matters. I can have an office prepared for you to work in, or you're welcome to stay here with me."

Hazel padded barefoot into the study, her feet cushioned by the thick cream-colored carpet. She eased into a chair opposite him on the other side of the desk. He slid her laptop toward her, then passed her a piece of paper with his network information. She logged into the secure network and spent the next hour checking her emails. It was thankfully a quiet few days, as Blake had guessed when he'd first told her she was to stay with him and Mason for a week. After an hour, she closed her laptop and leaned back in the chair, studying him.

"I loved watching you come on that boat with Mason's cock buried deep inside you," Blake murmured, as if he'd sensed the earlier direction of her thoughts. He closed his laptop and gazed at her across the expanse of his desk.

"You were watching us?" she asked.

"Yes. I saw the way he took you on that boat, how he tied up your pretty wrists and made you scream." His voice was low, silken, so dark and full of sin that her womb clenched with lust so hard it almost hurt.

Hazel's body quivered at the powerful memory. "How did you see us?"

He smiled, as if revealing a little secret. "Cameras. We have them all over the properties."

"So you saw . . ."

"*Everything* you did in the workshop." He leaned back in his own chair, his gaze deliciously dark, the blue of his eyes as fathomless as an ocean. Lord, she loved his eyes. They could tell her so much and yet hide everything at the same time. When he looked at her, he saw her in a way no one else ever had, except perhaps Mason. He seemed to see her the way Blake did too. In an instant, she envisioned what having a child with Blake might be like, a child who had his eyes . . . or a child who had Mason's smile? The thought filled her with a strange, wonderous sense of need that she'd never felt before.

"Do you want me, Hazel?" he asked quietly.

She took in the sight of him and how he looked so sexy and dangerous in those dark blue jeans, and how the faded T-shirt clung to his body. Mason made flannel and jeans look comfortable and sexy, but Blake in jeans and a T-shirt? Her feminine instincts warned her that it meant he was ready to get down and dirty in whatever way might please him. That sent a frisson of a thrill through her. This was a man who was obsessed with staying in control and never let his guard down, just like her. It was what made them connect—but also butt heads with each other at every turn. Perfect enemies, perfect lovers. He wondered if she wanted him? Of course she wanted him. She couldn't deny that.

Hazel nodded.

"How much do you want me?" Blake asked, his hands moving to rest on the arms of his chair. She swallowed, her mouth suddenly dry.

"I want you more than anything," she confessed in a whisper.

"Prove it to me. Show me what you want." He made no move. He simply waited like a wolf at the edge of the woods, its golden eyes fixed on a rabbit that it was hunting.

She was the rabbit, after all, one that wanted this wolf to hunt her. She stood and walked around the desk, and he slid his chair back a little, letting her sit on the edge of his desk facing him. He spread his legs slightly and rested his hands on his thighs, and she gazed at him a long moment before she got down on her knees and unfastened his jeans to free his hard cock. He remained motionless, his eyes still burning into her as he looked down at her.

She stroked the velvety shaft and then leaned forward to flick her tongue over the mushroom-shaped head. Her eyes darted up to his face, and she saw a tic work in his jaw as he fought off any reaction to her mouth on him. Emboldened by his attempt to conceal his emotions, she repeated the lick and took him into her mouth a few inches. She sucked hard and dragged the flat of her tongue along the underside of his cock. His hands clenched, white knuckles on the armrests. Hazel continued to lick and suck, trying out all the things she remembered he had liked. When his thighs started to tense and his hands curled into fists, she knew he was close. A feeling of delicious power surged through her at the thought of holding such control over this dominating man. The little rabbit had the wolf at her mercy. He cursed and his hips lifted, but before she let him find his release, she slid him free of her lips and stood up. She leaned over to whisper in his ear.

"Mason said I was bad today." She flicked her tongue in his ear. "He spanked me, but I think you know what I need, don't you, sir?" She knew what that would do to him.

Sir.

Both he and Mason responded in the same way to that one little word that carried so much weight to it.

"You say that word again, and you know what I'll do to you," he warned.

"Yes, *sir*," she replied, and shot him a look from beneath her lashes. It was time to break Blake's control.

Sir.

His sweet little rabbit knew just what to say to bring out the wolf in him. He stood, capturing her wrists behind her back before spinning her face down over his desk. He kept her there as he retrieved a pair of cuffs from his desk drawer and secured them around her wrists.

Then he linked the cuffs together to keep her wrists trapped at her lower back. He jerked the boxers she wore down past her ankles and removed them from her completely. He needed to get to her bare skin, to feel the slice of wet, hot heaven between her thighs. He nudged her legs wider apart and knelt behind her, his mouth seeking her wetness. He licked hungrily at her slit, tasting it until he was drunk on it. Her fingers flexed and curled as she reacted to his mouth. She whimpered and her legs started to shake, and that was his signal to stop.

He stood, licked his lips, and gazed down at her round, bare bottom on display.

"Please . . . sir." She begged for release.

He reached into his desk drawer and pulled out a tube of lubricant and drizzled it along the length of his cock before spreading it evenly. Then he spread Hazel's ass cheeks and pushed a lubed finger into her ass, testing her tightness before he added a second finger, making her wiggle and whimper as he stretched her. He took his time stretching her, wanting to prepare her so she wouldn't get hurt.

"Is this what you need?" he demanded in a low growl.

She nodded frantically, pushing her ass back at him in encouragement.

"Beg me to fuck your ass," he commanded.

Hazel tried to resist the direct order, and he added a third finger, spreading inside her until she shrieked and surrendered.

"Please, sir . . ."

"Please *what*?"

"Please fuck my ass . . . please." Her ragged panting and begging became his own private erotic symphony.

"Good girl," he murmured in praise and pulled his fingers out of her ass. He positioned the head of his cock there and began to push. He gave her ass a hard slap, which made her tense and relax, allowing him to sink in a few inches.

"You're doing so well," he praised again as he worked his way inside her inch by inch. "You were made to take me, weren't you, babe?" She was so tight, her muscles clamping down on his shaft, but he continued to work himself deeper and deeper.

"Please, sir, oh God . . ." She rested her cheek on the surface of his desk as he finally sank completely in and his balls slapped against her.

He stroked his hand over her hair before lightly digging his fingers into the locks. They breathed together for a few moments as she adjusted to the feel of him fully inside her. He had to give her time to stretch and accommodate him before he moved.

When she wriggled her bottom invitingly, he knew she was ready for him. He withdrew, spread more lube on his cock, and sank back into her ass again.

"That's it, take it like a good girl." He thrust deep, his balls tightening up as he drank in the sight of her prone form beneath him, her taking him inside her while he held on to her gorgeous auburn-red hair. He wrapped her hair around his fist and tugged lightly between slow, deep thrusts. Once he was certain she could take him harder, he began to pound into her. His desk creaked as he rammed his pelvis against the globes of her buttocks, and she rocked up on her tiptoes, her hands curled into tight fists. He grasped her cuffed wrists with his other hand, holding her prisoner as he fucked her like a man possessed.

"Sir . . . sir . . . sir . . ." She panted the word that drove him deeper into the darkest depths of his fantasies. If he could prove to her in this moment that she was his, truly his, that he would give her everything she needed, maybe she wouldn't leave, maybe she would stay . . . and let him love her.

Blake was beyond speech as the purest pleasure of taking Hazel like this swept over him, wiping his mind clean of sanity and his control. He was an animal, taking his mate, desperate to own everything, including her soul—just the way she already owned his.

"Good girl . . . good girl," he finally managed to say in a gruff voice as he continued to surge deep into her.

When she let out a scream of pleasure, she quaked beneath him, but he didn't stop. He kept pumping his hips. A few minutes passed, and he emptied himself into her ass. He let go of her hair and wrists so he could brace his hands on either side of her shoulders on the desk. Every part of him felt free and light, yet at the same time he struggled for breath. He'd been so rough with her, but she was smiling as she turned her head to look at him over her shoulder.

"You okay, babe?" he asked, his voice still rough as he regained his breath.

She nodded, closed her eyes, and continued to smile as she relaxed beneath him. His cock was still deep in her ass as he freed her wrists from the cuffs, and then he slowly pulled out of her. She whimpered, and he murmured a soft, soothing apology. His cum dripped out of the tight, puckered hole, and the sight of it made his cock bob again eagerly. He loved knowing he'd filled her.

He hastily used a Kleenex to wipe his cock before he tucked himself back into his pants. Then he took a moment to clean her up too before he scooped her up into his arms and settled in his chair with her on his lap. She still wore Mason's shirt but nothing else, and he knew she'd be cold soon enough. So he wound his arms around her back and along her thigh, lending her his own body heat. He let her lie back against him and rest. He'd had everything he'd ever wanted in life growing up except love, except someone who belonged to him. Even having Mason as a brother of sorts wasn't the same as this. Hazel was his world. His everything. His lips curved into a smile as he kissed her forehead.

He replayed the instant he'd first seen her. He'd been leaving their torts law class after receiving their grades on one of their papers. She'd been correcting their teacher about the assignment. The textbook had apparently been wrong, and so the professor had given them erroneous information to complete the paper. She had stood her ground, proud and unafraid as the professor tried to argue, but she won, giving the entire class extra points on their assignments. Blake had known in that moment he would find out who she was . . . and marry her.

That first night with her had changed his world forever. And now he had less than six days to convince her to stay. Hazel yawned against his chest and nuzzled his throat. He continued to hold her, and the weight of her felt perfect in his arms. When he was convinced she was asleep, he kissed her forehead again.

"You're mine," he vowed. "Forever."

Chapter Seven

Hazel spent the next several days in a blissful pattern of moving between the two houses and two beds, sharing herself with Blake and Mason each night. By day she worked in an office that Blake had set up for her, but she often took her laptop to Mason's workshop or Blake's office so she could work while being close to them. It gave her time to talk with them. It was easy to be with Mason and Blake, separately and the three of them together, even when they weren't having sex. There was no jealousy. They only occasionally teased her about being with one of them more often than the other. Their teasing often dissolved into the most delicious punishments that always turned to pleasure in the end. She was quick to learn that they both enjoyed finding reasons to call her a bad girl, which often resulted in a spanking or a deliciously hard fucking. But they always made it feel so good, and she always came screaming with an orgasm so strong she thought she might die from it. And what a great death that would be.

But now she was facing her last night with them. The week had gone by too fast. She could see the tension building in both Blake and Mason. Mason had warned her that he wouldn't let her leave, but Blake had said it was *her* choice. Was it? Could they keep her here if she decided she did want to leave?

As for herself, she felt certain she wanted to leave, but the thought of it made her taste acid. If this was her last night, she did want one thing from them. To be together, fully and completely. So far, they'd only taken turns being inside her. She wanted *more*. She wanted it all. She wanted what Blake had promised her, that she'd take them together.

Hazel dressed for dinner that night with care. She had forgone her jeans and instead wore one of her favorite pieces of lingerie. Chalmers had been given the night off, so it was only the three of them in the house. Therefore, she didn't mind parading around in lingerie. The black teddy she had put on was see-through, and the thong underwear, while uncomfortable, wouldn't be on long enough to annoy her.

As she reached the large kitchen, she heard Mason and Blake talking but couldn't hear the words clearly, just the comforting rumble of their deep voices. The kitchen table was set for three, the way she liked it. They never used the large formal dining room. Candles were lit on the table, and a serving of her favorite dish, chicken parmesan with angel-hair pasta, sat on each of the three plates. Her mouth watered at the sight. Mason must have cooked it for her to make this meal special.

She rubbed her chest, trying to ignore the sting she felt deep inside. She wasn't going to get emotional, not now. She had to focus on sex and her plan to seduce Blake and Mason into agreeing to the idea she'd come up with. She didn't want to let go of her own life or get too close emotionally to them, but she was convinced that if she came to them from time to time, on her terms, it could be great for the three of them. She cleared her throat, and both men turned to look her way. Mason's jaw dropped a little, and he let out a whistle. Blake's gaze seared her as his blue eyes raked over the lingerie and trailed along her bare limbs.

"Well now . . . ," he said, his tone sinfully dark.

"Forget the chicken parm." Mason set his beer down on the counter and started toward her, his hands flexing as though he ached to get his palms on her.

Blake thrust out an arm, halting Mason in place.

"Dinner first," he murmured to his friend. "Our girl needs to eat."

Mason shot Hazel a look that sent a wildfire of pure lust through her and made her want to forget dinner immediately.

"Fine, but the moment dinner's over, I'm taking her, Blake. No waiting." Mason's tone was hard and gruff, and she shivered in anticipation.

Feeling a swell of triumph, Hazel sat down at the table and pulled her chair forward. She waited for the men to join her. She had a proposal to make to them, and she wanted them to be so desperate for her that they would agree to her terms.

Mason and Blake sat down on either side of the table, leaving her at the head of the table so she could face them.

"Given how well this week has gone, I had an idea . . . a proposal, if you will."

"Proposal?" Blake arched a dark brow.

"Yes." She swallowed hard. "The three of us get along, so I thought we could make this a more frequent arrangement. Perhaps every couple of weeks I could come stay here with you."

"No," Blake uttered. His soft words felt like a slap.

"No?" she challenged. "Why not?" She glanced at Mason, who said nothing and looked toward Blake.

"Tonight you choose to stay with us or you choose to go. We aren't interested in casual relationships, are we, Mason?" Blake cut a look to his friend, who nodded in agreement.

"But I can't . . ." Hazel tried to calm her sudden rush of panic. "Blake . . . you know I need to be alone."

She couldn't stay, because if she did, she would fall in love with them, and when she lost them it would destroy her. Why couldn't Blake understand that?

"I told you six years ago that I couldn't lose someone I love ever again." She stood, feeling more than ever like a fool. He'd told her what her choices were. Why had she thought she could offer a third option? Because she'd always tried to negotiate every-thing in her life, that was why. It was what made her such a good lawyer . . . or so she'd thought. But now fresh doubts crept in about all aspects of her life. All these years she'd thought she'd won the battles against Blake fairly. But maybe he'd let her win, maybe he'd given her those frequent victories so that their game could continue like this. Had that part of her life been a lie?

"Why don't you sit and eat, Hazel. Then we can talk about this more," Mason said and reached for her hand.

She flinched. She couldn't have Mason touch her. If she did, it would make it hard to think.

"Right, Blake?" Mason asked. "Tell our girl to sit and eat her dinner."

The black pit of despair and pain grew in her belly. "I'm sorry, but I'm not hungry anymore." She stepped away from the table, and both men rose instantly to their feet. "I think it's time I left. I'm going to pack my things and call a cab." She fled the room, running all the way to Blake's bedroom, where she tore the stupid lingerie off and dressed quickly in jeans and a cable-knit sweater.

She had everything packed, including her laptop, and was halfway down the stairs when she noticed Mason was blocking her way. He stood at the bottom of the stairs, his arms crossed over his chest. He wore a gray henley with a few top buttons undone, revealing his throat and a bit of his chest. It was as if he knew her weakness. She longed to bury her face against his neck and feel his arms come around her and hold her until she felt safe. But that need? That was the thing that scared her. She couldn't afford to need anyone.

"Sweetheart," Mason said soothingly in that voice that could have gentled even the wildest of animals.

"No." She shook her head at him. "No, I have to leave."

"Why? It can't be because you lost your parents. Sweetheart, loss is a part of life. The hurt you feel when you lose someone? That means what you felt was real.

Grief is no less than the love lost that created it. What matters is how you grow around your grief."

She stared at him, knowing her gaze was hard, but she had to protect herself, had to protect her heart. "Let me go, Mason."

He moved, allowing her to walk past him. Even though letting her go was what she demanded of him, it didn't hurt any less that he did.

"Hazel."

She was reaching for the doorknob, but her hand froze when he spoke her name. She closed her eyes.

"He needs you to stay for the same reason you need to leave. You know that, don't you? You both fear the same thing . . . losing each other. The question is, would you rather live without him and hurt . . . or do you want to heal by staying with him?"

Tears blurred her eyes, and she refused to answer him. She pulled the door open and rushed outside to wait for her cab. When the door closed behind her, her shoulders drooped and her breath escaped in a slow, pained rhythm. Mason's words still echoed in her head.

Would you rather live without him and hurt . . . or do you want to heal by staying with him?

Blake stared at the kitchen table, his heart in his throat as his world crumbled around him.

"Blake, man." Mason roughly shook his shoulder. Blake blinked and lifted his dazed eyes up to his friend. "You have to go after her. Let her stay with us on *her* terms. But you have to tell her how you feel. She needs to know." Mason jerked his head toward the doorway behind him. "Go now, before we lose her."

Blake couldn't move, not at first, then he finally did. He ran for the door and flung it open. A car was driving away in the distance, and he watched the red brake lights flash briefly before the car turned onto the street and vanished around a corner. She was gone. He was too late because losing her had frozen him inside. His legs gave out beneath him, and he collapsed onto his backside on the steps leading up to his front door. He buried his face in his hands, trying to remember how to breathe when it felt like an avalanche had just collapsed on his chest.

Why hadn't he let her stay on her own terms? His stubbornness, his fear of losing her, had caused him to lose her forever.

"Blake?" A soft, pained voice came from behind him. He opened his eyes and turned to stare at the figure leaning against the wall just by his front door.

"Hazel." He breathed her name and realized he had

barreled past her where she stood somewhat hidden against the side of the house. Her bag sat at her feet, and she had her arms wrapped around herself.

Blake surged to his feet and went to her, pulling her into his embrace before she could protest. He needed to hold her, to feel her safely in his arms so that he didn't slip farther over the brink of madness. He cupped the back of her head and tucked her face into his chest.

"I'm sorry . . . I'm so damned sorry," he murmured over and over as he clutched her to him. "Stay with us on your terms. I can't lose you, Hazel. Please forgive me. I'm a stubborn asshole, but one who loves you with everything I have."

She said something, but it was muffled because of the way he was holding her. She finally lifted her head.

"Before you came out here, I'd already decided I wanted to stay with you . . . forever. I was just working up the courage to go back inside." She stared up at him with those lovely hazel eyes full of tears.

"You know I'd do anything for you," Blake said. "Anything."

She smiled up at him, and that single expression stole his very soul.

"I know. And I would do anything for you too." She leaned up on her tiptoes and kissed him. From the first moment he'd met Hazel, she'd been his *everything*, and in the six years they'd known each other, that had never changed.

"Dinner is still warm, if anyone's hungry," Mason announced calmly from the doorway. They both turned to look at him, and he grinned softly. "Everything all right, sweetheart?" he asked her.

Hazel nodded shyly at him. "Yes . . . and I think I'm hungry . . . again," she admitted with a laugh.

Blake put an arm around her waist as they walked through the door. No one wanted Mason's hard work preparing such a fabulous dinner to go to waste and get cold.

After the three of them finished dinner, Blake led Hazel upstairs to his room and Mason followed. Tonight they had made their choice, all three of them, and it was time to cement their bond in the best way possible.

Mason moved first, pulling Hazel into his arms and kissing her as though they had a thousand years to enjoy each other. Blake knew what it was like to kiss her like that, and what a gift it was. He knew just how she would melt into Mason's arms. Blake enjoyed the sight of his friend and the woman he loved kissing, more than he could say. It felt right. He and Mason were held together by their love for this incredible woman.

When Mason finally broke the kiss, he turned her to face Blake in a clear invitation to take his own kiss.

"Show him how much you love him, sweetheart," Mason encouraged her with a gentle push toward Blake, and then he began removing his shirt.

Blake pulled Hazel once more into his arms, their lips coming together as if carved by some ancient sculptor who had cut them from marble long ago.

We are the same, she and I, he thought. *Cut from the same stone.*

* * *

Mason dropped his shirt to the floor and unfastened his jeans but didn't remove them. He toed off his boots and socks, relishing the feel of the soft carpet beneath his bare feet. Then he crept up behind Hazel and slid his hands up under her sweater to stroke her belly and cup her breasts through the lacy bra she wore. She made a soft sound of delighted surprise against Blake's mouth, and Mason grinned.

He had been holding back this week, keeping his wildness under control, afraid to spook their girl, but now she was staying. She was theirs, and it was time he showed her what that meant. He unbuttoned the front of her jeans and gently tugged them down her legs. Blake moved at the same time, capturing her wrists at the small of her back. Her panties came off next, and

Mason tossed them away. He moved close behind Hazel, sliding one hand between her legs to stroke the slick folds of her sex. She trembled as he penetrated her slowly, letting her feel his fingers as he played with her. Wetness began to coat his fingers, and she clenched her legs tight around him. She was ready. She met Blake's gaze as the other man lifted his head from Hazel's.

Mason gave him a nod, and Blake moved backward, falling onto the bed. He took Hazel with him so she lay on top of him. She squeaked at the sudden movement, but Blake distracted her with another kiss. She still wore her sweater and bra, but Mason didn't mind—he had access to what he needed. Her pretty bottom was at the perfect height for him. He freed his cock and rubbed the tip of it along the wet seam of her sex and coated himself in Hazel's arousal. Then he pushed into her. It was hard not to just surge deep, but he kept his control, letting her adjust to his size and sudden invasion. Then he rocked his hips, his eyes almost rolling into the back of his head as he felt her inner walls grip him and squeeze.

"That's it, sweetheart, grip my cock," he growled as he surged deep in her again, making her whimper against Blake's mouth. He fucked her slowly, taking his time, but he didn't let himself come. When he felt she was close to coming, he pulled out of her and tapped

Blake's knee with one hand—the signal that they would share her together now.

Blake shifted his hips, moving Hazel up the bed a bit. He undid his own jeans and thrust into Hazel's wet heat. She let out a little cry of pleasure, and Blake held still, letting her adjust to the sudden invasion.

Mason retrieved the tube of lube from the nightstand and drizzled it against the puckered hole of Hazel's ass, working one well-coated finger inside her. He and Blake had worked on stretching her ass all week, and now would be the true test. Could she take them both?

He pressed against her entrance, pushing in inch by inch as she gasped and parted, taking him little by little. He could feel Blake's cock through the inner wall that separated them. When Mason was finally, *fully* inside her, she was panting hard and moaning. Blake released her wrists, and she braced herself on his chest, staring down at him wide-eyed. Mason wanted to be beneath her next time, wanted to see her face as she was completely filled by them.

"Good girl," Mason praised gruffly. She gasped at his praise as he stroked a hand over her hair before he gripped her waist. Blake held the globes of her lush ass, and the two of them moved in perfect tandem. One slid in and the other slid out while she wriggled, groaned, and trembled between them, taking them as they moved faster and harder. Mason wanted to stay buried in Hazel's body forever, to never let her leave this bed, such was the exquisite feeling of taking her like this.

His thrusts grew almost punishing as he let go of his fears and worries. She wasn't leaving, she was staying. She was *his*. He and Blake shifted their rhythms, matching their thrusts into her at the same time, and it sent their good girl off like a grenade. She screamed and tensed, her body clamping down on both their shafts so hard Mason sucked in a harsh breath.

"Fuck!" Blake roared, and Mason couldn't speak. He emptied himself into Hazel's ass, his vision blurring as he felt his entire body reduced to one infinite point of joy and pleasure.

When he came back to himself, he was still buried balls-deep in Hazel, and she collapsed on Blake's chest, her soft pants reaching Mason's ears. Blake's hand stroked her back in soothing patterns as he murmured soft things that made their girl smile, and she closed her eyes.

Mason trailed his own fingers over her spine then down over her ass and along her thighs as she shifted, getting more comfortable. He grinned. Only this girl would fall asleep with two men still inside her.

Mason withdrew, and she still didn't stir. He

cleaned himself off in the bathroom, stripped out of his jeans and briefs, and returned to the bed. Blake then let him take Hazel into his arms so that Blake could climb off the bed and take care of himself. Mason removed Hazel's sweater and bra, and she murmured something drowsily but let him strip her.

When Blake rejoined them, sandwiching Hazel between them, she finally woke up a little and looked between Blake and Mason, her eyes playful but tired.

"Happy anniversary," she said with all the contentedness of a sleepy kitten.

* * *

Hazel couldn't help but grin up at the two men who'd stolen her heart six years ago.

Mason laughed, and Blake rolled his eyes. "This was one hell of a game this year," Mason said. "I almost thought for a minute you might actually leave us."

She put a hand on Blake's heart and then on Mason's. "I would never leave you," she vowed to them. "Never. I'm yours."

"We know." Blake nuzzled her neck and placed a soft kiss there.

She cuddled between the two men, marveling over how intense their anniversary week had been. Every year they played a game, taking turns as to whose fantasy they would play out. No matter how the game began, it always ended with love and devotion between the three of them. She'd lost so much in her life so early on that she needed to remind herself every year that she was blessed to love and be loved by Blake and Mason. It had been her idea to start the role-playing games as a way of reaffirming the love they shared.

This year had been her turn. She'd given it a lot of thought, and when she'd made her decision, she'd outlined her plan for the two of them. She wanted to be fought over at the bar, then rescued, only to be kidnapped and shared between them. She'd wanted to be at their mercy, feel like she'd been gifted to Blake and given to Mason. That fantasy of hers had been inspired by the night she and Blake had first made love while in law school.

She had beaten him at the moot court competition and agreed to get a drink with him. One thing had led to another, and they'd ended up back at his apartment. It was obvious from their first kiss that what lay between them was explosive. He'd taken her to places she'd never dreamed of with his passion and shown her what she'd really wanted from a lover. But as she lay contented in his arms, they both heard a door open. A blond-haired man the same age as Blake stood in the bedroom doorway watching them with hooded, lustful eyes. Blake peeled the sheets off her still sweat-dewed body and offered her to the other man. They'd taken her between them, pleasuring her until she thought she'd die from it. That was the first night she'd met Mason, the first night she'd been shared between them.

The chemistry had been explosive, but more than that, the love that had come so easily, so quickly between her and her two men had been astounding. But it had always been terrifying to feel so much for both of them so fast. She'd fled the next morning, determined to keep her distance, to never trust her heart, but damn them . . . she couldn't stay away. She belonged with these two men as surely as they belonged with her.

So she'd done the crazy thing and gone back to them. With her heart on her sleeve, she'd walked into Blake's apartment to find both men desperate to know where she'd gone. Blake jerked her into his arms, holding on to her as if she were the very air in his lungs, and Mason quietly smiled and took his turn holding her once Blake felt able to let her go. It was impossible not to trust that kind of love, the love that bound them so deeply together that fear had no place left in their hearts.

Next year it would be Mason's turn, and Hazel knew he had plenty of ideas of how he wanted their anniversary to go, but things were changing, and soon they would all face a far different future. Sometimes it was hard to imagine she'd been crazy enough in love to marry Blake just a few months after sleeping with him and Mason, or that she'd had a private ceremony with Mason just outside his home by the lake to tie herself to him too.

The three of them had been inseparable ever since, and while Hazel wasn't Mason's wife on paper, she was as married to him in her heart as she was to Blake.

"I think it's time we told Blake about your anniversary present," Mason said as he traced circles on her bare shoulder. She looked up at him, her nerves suddenly spiking. "Go on, sweetheart. Tell him."

Hazel rolled over to face Blake, and his gaze searched hers for answers, but he didn't press her to speak right away.

"I . . . um . . . so you know that Mason has been working on some special projects for clients?" Hazel said as she brushed a lock of dark hair back from Blake's blue eyes, and his worried expression softened.

"Yes," Blake said slowly, showing patience even as she danced around the subject.

"Just tell him, sweetheart," Mason encouraged.

Hazel swallowed. "Well, one of those special clients is *me*."

"You?" Blake still wasn't following.

"Yes. Mason has been building a cradle . . . for me."

"Why would—" Blake halted himself, his eyes going round as he realized what she was saying. "You're pregnant?" Blake breathed.

"*We're* pregnant," she corrected. "We're going to be parents."

Blake's eyes darkened with emotion, and he looked at Mason, who continued to smile. A child. The thing they'd all been wanting. It was finally the right time.

"How long have you known?" Blake demanded.

"Three months. It's still early, but I wanted to be sure before I got your hopes up. Mason figured it out sooner, otherwise I would have told you both at the same time." She'd been worried he'd be upset by that, but he seemed too happy to be mad.

Blake pulled her into his arms, kissing her soundly.

"We'll be careful. No more role-playing. We'll—" Blake began.

"Hush." Hazel placed a finger on his lips. "It's fine. *I'm* fine. We can still have our special anniversaries—we might just need to have a babysitter." She laughed softly, and Blake relaxed.

"Are you feeling all right? Mason and I can get a little rough. I don't want to hurt you or the baby."

"I'm okay. I promise I'll let you know when to go

easier. But right now, the best thing you can do is just love me . . . both of you."

"Forever," Mason and Blake said at the same time. She knew with all her heart they would.

Thank you for reading *A Sinful Gift*! More Emma Castle books will be coming soon! In the meantime, check out my other available titles at www.emmacastlebooks.com or explore my other romantic books under my other sexy penname Lauren Smith at www. laurensmithbooks.com

About the Author

Emma Castle has always loved reading but didn't know she loved romance until she was enduring the trials of law school. She discovered the dark and sexy world of romance novels and since then has never looked back! She loves writing about sexy, alpha male heroes who know just how to seduce women even if they are a bit naughty about it. When Emma's not writing, she may be obsessing over her favorite show Supernatural where she's a total Team Dean Winchester kind of girl!

Join Emma's Private Reader Group "Emma Castle's Crew" here: https://www.facebook.com/groups/429283600812685/

facebook.com/EmmaCastleBooks

instagram.com/emmacastlebooks

bookbub.com/authors/emma-castle

tiktok.com/@laurenandemmabooks